SUSPECT
A CONFESSIONAL ANTHOLOGY

Published by PHE Ink – Writing Solutions Firm
9597 Jones Rd #213
Houston, TX 77065

PHE Ink and the portrayal of the quill feather are trademarks of PHE Ink.

All characters and events in this book are fictitious, and any resemblance to actual person, living or dead, is purely coincidental.

The cataloging-in-publication data is on file with the Library of Congress.

Library of Congress Control Number:

ISBN: 978-1-935724-08-7 Print
ISBN: 978-1-935724-59-9 eBook

Copyright © 2012 by PHE Ink – Writing Solutions Firm

All Rights Reserved

Printed in the United States of America

April 2012

Genre: Anthology

FOREWORD

I had never read an anthology of any kind before reading SUSPECT: A CONFESSIONAL ANTHOLOGY and wasn't quite sure what to expect. I can tell you this book has taken me on an exhausting journey where each and every emotion was touched and awakened. I literally cried for some of the characters, and harbored hatred for others. I even, at times, wanted to scream out warnings to a few.

Dwelling on our sins can eat us alive. The memories will consume our lives if we allow them to, and sometimes they can destroy us completely. The Trinity Church in Portsborough, New York, is the chosen place for those searching for peace at Christmas.

They come with their burdens of rape, child abandonment, prostitution, murder and vengeance. Some come looking to confess their sins, and others come seeking redemption, and forgiveness. And then there are those that come to make peace the only way they see fit...through revenge.

I love SUSPECT: A CONFESSIONAL ANTHOLOGY because there is a bit of every one of us in the stories. Something we all can identify with. The authors involved in writing the anthology are serious story tellers, with a keen sense of human tragedy, commitment, redemption, and forgiveness.

> You'll never see Christmas quite the same.

Awesome job Linda Watson, LM Blakely, JA Gardner, Lorita Kelsey-Childress, Jean Holloway, C. Highsmith-Hooks, Michele T. Darring and TL James. What a ride!!

Author B. Grovner
Author of EVEN NUMBERS, COLD CRAZY & COLD SERIAL

TABLE OF CONTENTS

PLAY ME BY LINDA WATSON

SA'RAI BY LM BLAKELY

STATE STREET BY JA GARDNER

DOUBLE TAKE BY LORNA KELSEY CHILDRESS

IN THIS LIFE BY JEAN HOLLOWAY

MURDER IN THE SANCTUARY BY G. HIGHSMITH HOOKS

A WALK IN THE COURTYARD BY MICHELE T. DARRING

THE ESCORT BY TL JAMES

CHRISTMAS EVE
Trinity Episcopal Church
Portsborough, NY 2000

PLAY ME
LINDA WATSON

CHAPTER ONE

Lacy pulled up two cars behind Alexander's BMW in her compact Honda rental. This rental was something she would have never been seen in on a normal day, but she wanted to be discrete and ensure he wouldn't notice her. Today, she was prepared to put an end to all of his mistreatment and infidelity. She sat there patiently, thinking about how he had cornered her two days earlier and threatened to have her dragged into the streets if she didn't leave. She knew then that she didn't love him anymore.

With their assets in both names, she knew she would be financially secure and better off leaving him. Lacy was tired of being disrespected by Alexander, tired of all of his lies. She was prepared to put an end to it once she caught him red-handed. She sat unusually still, hoping not to bring any attention to herself and that no one could hear the uncontrollable pounding of her heart. She watched him get out of his car and head toward Trinity Episcopal Church. She watched as he looked around to ensure no one was following him and then rushed into the church. *Why is he going into that church? Really Alexander, meeting women in the church? Man, you have reached an all-time low.*

It was the cold of winter in Portsborough, NY and most people were busy trying to complete last minute Christmas shopping, but luckily, the church sat off on a side street in seclusion, away from all of the busy traffic. Lacy waited a few minutes and then pulled her dark brown hat down on her head. She put on her sunglasses, not only to hide her identity but also to hide the purple and blue ring that encircled her bruised eye from Alexander's fist. Lacy hopped out of the car and headed toward the church. As soon as she opened its doors, she noticed Alexander going into the confessional. She quickly scoped out the entire church, realized all of the pews were empty. She quietly ran toward the confessional to be in eavesdropping distance.

Lacy could hear voices as she drew closer to the confessional. She couldn't make out what was being said, but she knew one of the voices belonged to Alexander. He was arguing with someone who sounded like a woman, but it could have been a man. It was hard for her to tell.

He done lost his damn mind, how dare he sit his ass up in this confessional with another woman? I got his ass now and there's no way he'll get out of this one.

Fear began to take over her entire body. *Something just wasn't right.* She kept hearing someone say *Robert*, but Alexander would respond. Then she heard Alexander say, "This is going too far. I didn't sign-up for this. I'm not going to kill anyone." The male-female voice answered, "Robert, you have no choice, you must follow through with the plan."

Lacy was more confused than ever.

"I can't do it, I'm not going to," she heard Alexander say.

"Look Robert, if you don't do it first, then you'll be risking your life. There is no turning back, you're in too deep," the other voice said.

"Look, I have to go before she suspects something," Alexander answered.

Why does he keep calling him Robert? Oh my God, is he going to kill me? I knew it! Lacy ran out of the church before Alexander could leave the confessional, hopped in her car and drove away.

§§§

She drove around in circles trying to figure out what she heard and realized she had been with a man whom she may not even know. Many questions ran through her mind. *Who is Robert? Why did someone want him to kill me? Was this a setup from the beginning?*

Too afraid to go home, Lacy drove over to a courtyard a block away from the home she shared with Alexander parked, taking some time to think. After an hour, she slowly pulled off in the rental to go home. She realized she had to pack a few things and leave. Lacy parked around the back hoping she could sneak in through the basement and grab some clothes without him hearing her.

While frantically throwing clothing into a bag, Lacy could hear movement and voices above her head.

"How did you find me? I told you I'm done with this shit. It's over. You need to leave," she heard Alexander say as she eased her way to the top of the stairs. She then heard a rumbling sound.

"No, no, stop, don't, don't," Alexander pleaded. Then she heard two gunshots. Her heart was pounding so fast she couldn't think straight. She stood there, gripping the door handle, too afraid to enter. Finally, after being in shock for minutes, she opened the door and found Alexander lying there in a pool of blood. It was pouring from his head and mouth and he was gasping for his last breath.

Lacy fell to her knees, landing directly in the pool of blood. "Oh my God, Alexander, Alexander," were the only words she could manage to say.

Alexander opened his eyes and rolled them toward her. "Lacy, help me. I've been shot."

There were still people in the house. Lacy could hear them talking and rambling in her upstairs bedroom. Afraid for her life, she frantically ran down the basement stairs, almost taking a brutal fall, but she managed to collect herself. The stumble must have gotten their attention because she could hear them coming toward her. She immediately grabbed her bag, ran to the car and drove away.

§§§

Lacy was in shock as she headed toward the police station. Finally, she was able to pull herself together and think straight. She began to process the whole situation. *Lacy, remember Alexander's conversation at the church? This was the man who wanted to throw you out in the streets and he was planning to kill you. And let's not forget Robert. Who the hell is Robert? You really don't know this man or what he's involved in and why someone wants to kill him. Now you're covered in his blood, explain that to the police.*

She decided to call instead. She pulled out her cell phone and dialed 911. *Three years with a man I loved dearly, she thought, but now he's dying and I feel no remorse for him. Sorry God, but I only feel happy, free and thankful.* "I need an officer to go to my home, my boyfriend has been shot."

"A shooting? Where?" asked the officer.

"At my home, 21272 Delaware Avenue, in Portsborough" replied Lacy. Even she could hear the panic in her voice.

"Okay, please calm down. What's your name, Miss?"

"My name is Lacy Williams. I'm his girlfriend."

"Are you at the home now, Miss?"

Lacy's voice became rushed. "No, I'm not at home. I left. There was someone there and when they heard me they starting coming after me? I ran! I feared for my life."

"Slow down, Ms. Williams. Does this boyfriend of yours have a name?"

"Alexander...Alexander Sanders. He's dead! I know it. I was in the basement. I heard noises and when I came upstairs, I found him lying on the floor in a pool of blood."

"Ms. William, where are you now?"

"I'm headed to my sister's house on the south side."

"Can we call you if we have additional questioning?"

"Yes, my cell number is 212-777-9911."

"We're sending a car over there now."

CHAPTER TWO

Alexander was a lady's man. Being faithful to one woman wasn't part of his game plan. Alexander loved women and he had many. But the main four were Lacy, the live-in, Barbara, the executive who enjoyed buying Alexander expensive things, Shonna, the high-priced prostitute who loved making money for him, and Marilyn, the Caucasian banker who would do anything for Alexander, even embezzlement.

Lacy, his main woman, shared a home with him and was like his wife. Alexander met Lacy after being in New York for a year. He first laid eyes on her at a New York Giant's football game in the dead of winter. She was standing there on the fifty-yard line dressed in an Eskimo fur hooded coat. The fur hood on the coat that circled her round caramel face made her look so beautiful. At that moment, it seemed as if she was the only person there. It was love at first sight for Alexander. Even though he knew, he was in too deep with Barbara and her controlling ways he still had to have Lacy. So he promised her the world and delivered. He would have made Lacy his wife that very day. She was wife material - sweet, intelligent, and beautiful. But he couldn't involve her in any of his wrong doings. After two months of dating, they were living together. And because his job required travelling eighty-five percent of the time, Alexander knew he could live a double life without any of his women finding out.

Lacy's role was to clean, cook, and be at his 'beck and call' whenever he needed something. She realized a year into their relationship that she was the main one, but not the only one. And if she wanted to continue to be the main one, she would have to deal with all of his infidelity. In the beginning, she really didn't care because Lacy was being well taken care of and he treated her well. Until the very first night, he stayed away from home and didn't return until the following afternoon.

§§§

When he walked through the door, Lacy was in the kitchen preparing lunch. She heard the door slam and immediately ran to greet him.

"So where have you been all night? I've been worried sick about you. Couldn't even sleep because I thought something bad happened. Called your phone a million times and you wouldn't answer. Now you walk your ass in here today like everything's fine."

Alexander's whole demeanor changed and his golden completion darkened. "What did you say to me?"

"I said where the hell have you been?"

He got up in Lacy's face, spit flying. "I've been out fucking. That's where I've been. It's not the first time and won't be the last. As long as you live under my roof where I pay all the bills, feed and clothed your gold-digging ass, don't you ever question me again. You hear me, girl? If you even think about questioning me you can get the fuck out NOW." His tone got louder with each word.

He opened the door and indicated she could leave. Lacy turned around, walked back into the kitchen and continued to prepare lunch while tears rolled down her face.

She could hear Alexander ranting and raving all the way from the kitchen. "You ain't shit, never been shit. All you ever wanted from me was my money. You're worthless to me compared to my other women."

When Lacy heard "other women," she stormed back into the living room where Alexander was sitting on the Chenille fabric sofa having a shot of Martell Cordon Bleu. "Oh really! Other women now, Alexander?"

"Now? There have always been other women." Alexander took his hand and braggingly brushed his collar.

"I'm just good at what I do. You would've never found out. But it's time for you to know the truth because you have gotten beside yourself when you think you can question me. Guess what, Lacy?"

Lacy just stared blankly at Alexander. She couldn't believe what she was hearing.

Alexander hopped up from the sofa and walked over to Lacy and slapped her so hard blood pooled down the corner of her mouth. "I said guess what."

Lacy grabbed her face, afraid that if she didn't respond he would slap her again. "What, Alexander?"

"They all know about your ass and they don't say shit. They still give me whatever I want... money, clothes, pussy. And on top of that, they do whatever I say and don't complain about shit." Alexander was getting so good at lying he was beginning to believe it himself.

"Then there's your ass. I give you the world... treat you like a queen. You don't have to do anything but take care of me and this home. You don't work. We don't have children. You shop whenever you want to, travel wherever you want, hang out with those trifling ass girlfriends of yours...you do whatever the hell you want. And you have the nerve to nag and complain about everything. I've been too good to your ass. That's what it is. And the shit stops today or you can leave."

Alexander grabbed his Louis Vuitton leather jacket. "I'll be back in a few hours and if you're gone when I return, I don't give a fuck."

Crying, Lacy fell to the floor in a fetal position. She couldn't believe what just happened.

CHAPTER THREE

Alexander met Barbara Tomlin when he began his search for employment in New York. Fresh out of Harvard University sporting a Master's Degree in Economics He was new to the city and needed assistance obtaining work. Dressed in a white shirt, a pair of shabby worn black slacks and some black business shoes he picked up from Payless, he walked through the doors of Professional Recruiting Services. He checked out the joint in one minute flat. It was a small quaint office decorated with plants and a few abstract paintings on the wall. If Alexander didn't know any better, it looked like they had just opened for business, but that wasn't the case at all. They had been in business five years and he had heard many things about the company, some good and some not so good. Nevertheless, Professional Recruiting Services was one of the top financial recruiters in New York.

The receptionist area was located right at the door and two other desks located a few feet behind her. All three women that accompanied the desks were professionally dressed.

"Good Morning, my name is Alexander Sanders and I have a nine o'clock appointment with Wendy Weatherspoon."

"Sir, please have a seat. Ms. Weatherspoon will be with you shortly," the receptionist told him with a smile.

Alexander noticed a tall, beautifully mature woman come out of her office and walk toward a desk with the nameplate of Wendy Weatherspoon on it. He couldn't help but notice her since her big, black, stern eyes were glued to him the entire time. It made him uncomfortable.

Why the constant stare? I know she can see the puzzled expression on my face. Was that why she never once took her eyes off him? Alexander dropped his head and fingered through the pages of a Better Homes and Garden magazine he had grabbed from the table. He could hear her asking the other woman questions about his background. Then she grabbed the folder and began walking in his direction.

"Mr. Sanders?"

"Yes?"

"Good morning, I'm Barbara Tomlin, the owner of Professional Recruiting Service and I will be speaking with you today instead of Ms. Weatherspoon." She extended her hand and laid a handshake on him so firm it caused his circulation to stop. If he weren't looking directly at her, he would have sworn it was a man's grip.

Wow! She's powerful, strong and intimidating. One of the not so good things he had heard about Professional Recruitment Company was about the owner, Barbara Tomlin. She was not to be fucked with. "Good morning Ms. Tomlin, it's a pleasure to meet you."

She sized him up from head to toe with her nose in the air as if there was a foul odor circling in the room. "Please come with me, Mr. Sanders." They walked a few additional feet and landed in her office. She closed the door behind her. "Please have a seat."

"Ms. Tomlin, first I want to say thanks for taking time out of your busy schedule today to meet with me. I'm well aware of you and your success in the business, so you know I'm wondering why I'm getting the red carpet treatment?"

She crossed her legs and sternly glared at him over her gold-encrusted Versace designer glasses. "Mr. Sanders, the only reason you're receiving red carpet treatment from me today is because I'm impressed with your resume. A black man graduating with honors from Harvard University. Hmm, very impressive. And by the way, when interviewing with my clients don't you dare be so direct with them like you were with me just now."

"No, I apologize. I didn't mean anything by it. Believe me, I'm honored."

"Boy, you got a lot to learn about the corporate world."

I know she didn't just call me a boy, but don't dare say anything because I can't blow this opportunity.

"Yes, Ms. Tomlin."

She leaned back in her chair and laughed. "See what I'm talking about. When you should respond, you don't. I just called you a boy and your response was 'Yes, Ms. Tomlin?' Boy, you are so naïve."

Alexander felt more confused than ever. "Look, Ms. Tomlin, I may be fresh out of school and you're right, I know nothing about the corporate world, but if you can help me I'll greatly appreciate it."

"Great, I'm going to teach you some things that will guarantee your success. Just trust me. Let's go."

"Let's go, go where?"

"Are you going to trust me or not?"

"What about the interview?"

"It's just beginning." Ms. Tomlin grabbed her ten-thousand dollar red vermillion Hermes purse, pulled out her keys, opened the office door and walked out with the perplexed Alexander trailing behind.

§§§

They hopped in her gold Mercedes-Benz S64 AMG and headed north to Fifth Avenue. When they arrived at Saks, she went straight to the men's suit department.

"Hello, Ms. Tomlin, how are you today? It's good to see you again. How can we help you," asked the eager sales associate.

"Hi, Kathy, first you need to take his measurements. We're in the market for business suits today and put a move on it."

Alexander noticed how condescending Ms. Tomlin was when speaking to the sales associate, but he ignored the signs.

Ms. Tomlin pointed toward the sales associate walking away. "Alexander, you can go with her."

"Yes, Ms. Tomlin."

"Barbara, call me Barbara."

"Okay, yes, Ms. Barbara."

Alexander could see her pulling suits from different sections in the designer area. She had the sales associates running around like she was the richest woman in the world. Barbara grabbed the suits from the saleswoman and walked toward him.

"Here, try these on."

Once in the dressing room, Alexander glanced down at the price tags on the suits that range from six hundred to fifteen hundred dollars by designers he had never heard of, like John Varvatos Star USA, Boss and Joseph Abboud.

His eyes grew big as saucers. *I don't know why she brought me in here. I can't afford these suits.*

"Come out, Alexander, so I can see how they look on you."

He strutted out of the dressing room, walking like a model in a fashion show.

"Hmm, that looks good on you. I'll take it." Barbara ended up buying five suits totaling over five thousand dollars. "Please charge these to my corporate account, Kathy."

Kathy smiled and shook her head. "Will do, Ms. Tomlin."

"Now off to the next spot, Alexander," Barbara commanded.

"Ms... I mean Barbara, why are you buying these things for me? I can't afford any of them. I don't have a job, remember?"

"Don't worry Alexander, you'll get the job. I have a company looking for bright, young, talented black men. You'll be meeting with them tomorrow. Starting pay there will be at least six figures. You can pay me back after you land this sweet job."

By the time the day was over Barbara had spent an additional five thousand dollars on shoes, shirts, ties, cuff links, cologne and even a haircut for Alexander. He felt like a kid in a candy store. He had hit the jackpot.

"Do you treat all of you clients this way, Barbara?" She glared over her glasses. "No, only the ones that are a good investment and don't get this twisted, Mr. Sanders, I want all of my money back." She quickly pulled up to O'Casey's, a pub near Saks. "We're going here for dinner and I can give you some pointers on how to conduct yourself during the interview."

The waitress sat them at a table that had a view of Fifth Avenue and handed them two menus.

"I will be right back with water and to take your orders."

Barbara nodded and began scanning the menu. The waitress reappeared with glasses of water in hand.

"We would like two mushroom burgers with Swiss cheese." She placed a hand on top of his. "I hope you like hamburgers. Their mushroom burgers are the best, you'll love it."

Damn, she's bossy...and a little annoying. But until he got the job, he wouldn't dare challenge her. He definitely didn't want to be on her bad side because he knew there would be hell to pay. Alexander couldn't afford that, besides he had to land that job.

"Yes, I do like burgers, Barbara. Thank you."

"Mary, can you bring us two glasses of your best red wine, please."

"Sure thing, Ms. Tomlin, I'll be back in a sec."

Dang and she knows everybody everywhere she goes and even though she talks down to them, they seem to like her, probably because of the tips she's giving.

They ate their burgers and after downing two carafes of wine, Barbara was becoming very friendly and familiar with him. The professional persona she started out with had completely changed. She was laughing, touching, flirting and talking about the fakeness of people in the corporate world and what he needed to do to play the game and get ahead. *Now I like this side of her! She really seem like she could be cool people.*

"I like you a lot, Alexander, I do and I want to see you make it. There are only a few African American men in corporate America who have gotten far. You know why that is, don't you?"

"No, actually I don't."

"Well, it's because the white man fears y'all. But you're likable. They're gonna love you." She let out a playful laugh, "And with your high yellow, 'damn near look white' complexion, you can pull it off. I promise you. Just play the game, their game, and you will win."

From out of nowhere, Barbara leaned over toward Alexander.

"I want you to spend the night with me."

Wow! Spend the night! Am I hearing correctly? She'd gone directly from talking about corporate America to asking him to sleep with her.

"Did you just ask me to spend the night with you?"

"Yes, I'm an old freaky lady who needs loving too. I want you to take up residency in my body tonight. You can have total control. Renovate it as you see fit. Do with it what you like. It's in need of an overhaul. Reconstruct it, if you want. Like I said baby, I'm an older woman and I'm going to teach you so much, although you look like you know how to please a woman. Just trust me. Okay?"

Even though Alexander wasn't feeling Barbara at all, he knew he had to play the game in order to win her trust and land the job. And he knew if he told her no, there was no chance in hell she would help him achieve what he wanted.

"Okay, Barbara, tonight I promise I'm going to do my best to make all of your fantasies come true."

CHAPTER FOUR

Although exhausted, the following afternoon he made the 3:00 p.m. appointment Barbara had scheduled for him and met with Mr. Geoffrey Brown, CEO of Brown Foster. Alexander felt he had not done his best, especially after Barbara kept him awake most of the night demanding to be pleasured over and over again. He was somewhat nervous, but he couldn't do any wrong that day. Everything went in his favor.

Mr. Brown wiped his hand across his balding head and leaned back in his seat until his belly protruded onto the desk.

"I like you, Alexander and Barbara likes you. She said you're a winner. That's good enough for me. I want you on my team. I'm putting together a team of top-notch traders and with your poise and intellect; you fit the bill. I hope you say yes because I'm telling you, you can make a lot of money. I'm going to start you out at eighty-five thousand, but you can make twice that amount this year if you want.

It's all up to you. This is your job, Alexander, if you want it," Mr. Brown coaxed.

Wow, a possible hundred and seventy thou this year? Sounds too good to be true, but I would be a damn fool to turn this down. Alexander stood and shook Mr. Brown's hand. "Thank you Mr. Brown, of course I accept your offer. It's better than my wildest dreams. Here I am fresh out of college, employed by one of the top financial companies in the world and starting out on the trading floor. That's a triple win situation for me. Sir, I'm honored."

$$$

Just as Barbara promised, Alexander landed the job with Brown Foster Investments and because of her, his life was never the same. Barbara and Brown Foster were tied into so many illegal wrong doings that he soon became intertwined in their dealings. Alexander found his life spiraling in a downward path into hell.

He realized he had made it at Brown Foster when Geoffrey invited him into their corporate Secret Society. Brown Foster was a company with a cultural environment that strived on being a winner. You had to do whatever it took to win and make the big bucks. Be it lying, cheating, stealing, killing or whatever. Alexander passed that portion of his new hire training with flying colors after Mr. Brown asked him to fudge numbers on several accounts. He was fine with it as long as Mr. Brown was the one signing off and his name wouldn't appear on anything.

$$$

Alexander had been working at Brown Foster for two years when he met Shonna. It was his first initiation into their secret society during a confidential business meeting scheduled by the CEO, Geoffrey Brown. They held the meeting outside of the office at a secret location. The five traders. Alexander and four other guys who were all Caucasians, met at a private location on Rush Street. They drove around to the back of the building where Mr. Brown was waiting.

"Hi guys, you're right on time. Now I have great trust and confidence in my team. The last two years has shown that and I owe it all to you five here. To show my appreciation for your loyalty I have a treat for all of you."

The six men walked up to the door where a tall, burly, black dude greeted them. "Good afternoon Mr. Brown, I'm happy to see you back. Are these guys with you?"

"Yes, Larry, they're with me."

"Now you know the routine."

"Yes, they're okay with it."

"Okay, guys, please hand over your briefcases, phones, identification and step through the door."

"Why is this necessary?" Alexander asked.

Mr. Brown angrily glared over at him and gave him a 'shut up and do what they say' look. Alexander handed all of his personal items to the guy without another word.

A curvaceous black woman who looked like she could be Beyoncé's twin sister, walked up to them and placed blindfolds over their eyes. Alexander, along with the other traders, began to drool as excitement took over. Alexander could feel someone grab his hand and lead him down a walkway. He heard a door open and then he was pulled through it and then heard the door shut.

"Hello, my name is Shonna," a soft female voice said.

"Hello," said Alexander.

"I'm going to sit you down in this chair."

"Okay."

"I'm here to give you pleasure, whatever you want I will do and Mr. Brown said give you whatever you want."

With all of the false accounts he had set up, embezzlement, stealing, bribery and now this, Alexander found himself spiraling deeper and deeper down a dark path with Mr. Brown and Brown Foster. As promised, Alexander doubled his salary the first year and was now making over a half million dollars; however his earning were all based on illegal dealings. He realized money brought many things, even power. The money and power changed Alexander. He became more and more like Mr. Brown and enjoyed every moment.

"So, Mr. Brown said you can give me whatever I want?" Shonna begin to massage Alexander's entire body.

"Yes, whatever you want. He pays well." Alexander gripped Shonna ass tightly in his hands.

"Well Shonna, do you have a friend? I've never been with more than one woman at a time."

"I have many friends, what do you prefer; male, female, white, black, Asian? It's all up to you."

Just the thought of Alexander getting what he wanted aroused him. "Damn, I like this shit. Okay, I want two more women to accompany you, one white and one Asian."

"Not a problem. So, do you have a name?"

"Yeah, call me Al."

"Okay, Al. I will be right back. Sip on this until I return."

Shonna handed him a glass and it smelled like Hennessey. He began to take slow sips from the glass and started feeling nice and relaxed. Two minutes later, the door opened then closed. "Al, we're back. Would you like to see your choices?"

"Most definitely."

She gently removed his blindfold and he felt like he had gone to heaven. Standing before him were three beautiful women, completely naked and ready for action. But out of the three, he had to admit that Shonna was one bad, black sister. She knew how to work every part of her body. She licked him from head to toe.

"Oh, baby, damn, hmm, damn, that feels good. What the fuck? Damn baby, you know your shit."

Shonna had Alexander moaning and groaning which was not his norm. He was the one who made women scream, not the other way around, but she had his head spinning in a good way. Shonna also knew how to delegate. She told the other two girls what to do and how to do it and they did it well.

Alexander was star struck by Shonna. So star struck that he began seeing her once a week. He began to lose interest in Lacy and Barbara. Strangely, Shonna was falling for him too. He didn't realize how much until one late night while they were lying in bed together after a strenuous workout when she brought it up.

"Alexander, I want to be yours and only yours. I like the way you make me feel."

He already had a difficult time juggling Lacy, Barbara and Marilyn and did not have the time to date another woman, especially with Barbara and Marilyn demanding more time with him. There was no way.

"Girl, I like you too, but I think that's against the rules. I can't go messing things up."

"Look Al, no one has to know. I will leave this business and we can live together."

He had to come up with a fast lie. "HELL NO! That wouldn't work, Shonna. Geoffrey comes by my home all the time for meetings. Noooo, that wouldn't work. Besides, I travel most of the time, so living together isn't a likely option." He kissed her on the forehead. "Let's keep it the way it is, okay?"

Shonna returned his kiss except she moved down and touched her lips to the area between his navel and his groin. That gave him uneasy feeling and he squirmed away from her.

"We can both leave our jobs and start an upscale escort service someplace else. I'll make you more money than you have ever seen." Alexander looked puzzled.

"Work for me? What do you mean by that, girl?"

"I mean, I like you and I will sell my ass for you and bring you every dime."

He hopped up from the bed. "What?"

"You heard me baby. I didn't stutter."

"Damn girl, you'd do that for me? I don't know anything about that shit! I'm a business man but it's definitely not that kind of business."

"I'll teach you everything. You can make big money. More than you've ever seen. You'd be amazed what these white corporate freaks pay for pretty black girls. I have some loyal customers who will fly me all over the country just to be with them. It can all be yours as long as you're with me."

Alexander knew a good offer when he saw it. He couldn't refuse the proverbial one.

CHAPTER FIVE

Marilyn sat next to Alexander as he watched her nervously bite down on her fingernails. This always annoyed him. "Baby, I think they're on to me because they want to conduct an audit in my department next week. I don't know what to do," she confessed.

"What do you mean they are on to you? You mean to tell me you didn't cover your ass?" This annoyed him even more.

Marilyn hopped up from the sofa and began to pace the floor. "Well, with me being a loyal 'white' manager for over twenty years, I never thought they wouldn't trust me. I doctored all of the reports."

"What? You're dumber than I thought. I don't know why I ever fucked with you. You got this game twisted if you thought your *white* ass was untouchable."

§§§

Alexander met Marilyn a year after he started at Brown Foster. Their relationship started out as business, but a month later, she was inviting him to her goods. She was a spontaneous woman. That's what he liked about her. She would drop her drawers anywhere. The first time they had sex was in her office on the floor behind her desk. Then there was a time when she threw him across the front hood of her Mercedes in the middle of the afternoon and began to perform oral sex on him while people walked by. There were so many exciting moments Alexander lost count of all the times she jumped his bones. He didn't understand why she seemed so sex-starved. Maybe it was the fact she had never had a Black man before or because of all the powder she sniffed up her nose.

§§§

He watched her shake some white powder from a small plastic bag onto her dining room table. She then made two perfect lines using her business card and grabbed a straw from the table. Marilyn snorted a line of powder into each nostril. She became extremely jittery and began to speak at a rapid pace.

"They've never questioned me before. Maybe it's just a routine audit."

Alexander grabbed the plastic bag off the table and held it in front of her. "Here's your problem. This white dust is controlling you. That's why you've been slipping and everyone on your job is noticing the change in your behavior."

Her eyes were as big as saucers. "I don't want to hear that shit, Alexander. Bring your ass over here and let me kiss on your strong body."

"You just don't get it, do you girl? You're about to be audited and all you can think about is sex. I'm done. I'm out of here." He grabbed his coat from the coat rack sitting in the corner by the door.

"Wait, what do you mean you're done and you're out of here?"

"I'm not going down for you, Marilyn. You're getting very sloppy with the way you're handling things these day and I'm not going to be a part of it."

"Wait, baby, you have no choice. You're in this as deep as I am. If I go down, guess what, you're going down too. Remember you spent more of that money than I did."

Alexander walked over to Marilyn and grabbed her by her neck. "What did you say?"

"You heard me, baby. If I go down, then so will you."

"Your pitiful threats don't scare me. I'm nobody's fool. You'd have to get up early in the morning to get me caught up in your bullshit. You can't prove you ever gave me one single dime, lady. You won't find my name on one single document you used to embezzle money from your bank. Now if you want to bring Mr. Brown into your world of corruption, I suggest you reconsider because you would be getting in way over your head. On that note, I'm out and you can lose my number."

Marilyn stood in front of him blocking the door. "Wait Alexander, don't leave, I didn't mean..."

"Look, I don't take kindly to threats. Now get out of my way." Alexander left her home, slamming the door behind him. He could hear Marilyn screaming from the other side.

"You're gonna pay Alexander, I promise you that."

CHAPTER SIX

After the threats from Marilyn and all of the illegal dealings at the company, accepting the role of pimp that Shonna gave him, Alexander realized he was a country boy gone bad. He was in way over his head. He had grown up on a farm in Memphis, Tennessee, raised by two strict parents who instilled great values. But after graduating college with honors and joining Brown Foster, everything changed for him. In a deep mess with no way out, he can hear his parents saying, *"Everything that seems too good to be true usually is."* He needed a plan to protect himself. Even though he very careful about anything being traced back to him, he still needed a better security blanked. He pulled out his private cell phone and dialed Shonna's number.

"Hello."

"Hey, baby, it's Al. I need you to do me a favor."

"Anything for you, baby."

"Shonna, remember you told me all of the secret society rooms are bugged and the tapes are hidden? Well, I need a copy of the tape with Mr. Brown and his two Black burly friends in one of his dominatrix acts."

"What?"

Alexander sensed the confusion in Shonna's voice. "Yes, baby, I need you to do me this one favor. I think Brown Foster is about to go down, and I'm not going down with them. I need some insurance."

"You know I'll do anything for you, but this may be difficult for me to pull off."

"Shonna, you're clever. I know you can get the tape."

"Yeah, but what's in it for me?"

Another call came in on Alexander's phone. "Hold on baby, I have another call." He clicked over. "Hello."

"Alexander, this is Marilyn. Why are you avoiding me? You think I'm playing with your ass? I'm going to..."

Alexander immediately switched back to the other line. "Shonna?"

"Yes."

"I'll give you four hundred thousand to get the tape. I will bring you the money tomorrow."

Shonna laughed. "Well, that certainly will do it. Are you okay, Al?"

"Yes, but I gotta go. Have to handle this other call. I'll see you tomorrow." Before Shonna could say goodbye, Alexander had switched over to his other line. "Look, Marilyn, don't call this number again. I'm..." Another call came through so Alexander switched over to his over line before Marilyn could say a word. "Hello?"

"Hello, Alexander?"

"Who is this?"

"This is Barbara, Who did you think it is? Are you alright?"

"Oh, hey Barbara, I thought you were someone else."

"Who, another woman? Is that why you have no time for me now? After everything I've done for your black ass, now you want to ignore me because you have another woman?"

"Look Barbara, I don't have another woman, so you need to stop tripping. I'm going to hang up on your ass if I have to deal with this shit. I have enough stress dealing with work."

Alexander felt stressed out because Barbara was becoming extremely jealous, demanding, violent and threatening. He knew Mr. Brown was telling her his every move, when he was in town and when he was traveling. She couldn't understand why he wasn't spending more time with her. She started following him; it couldn't be a coincidence that they kept running into each other. He began staying at one of the company's downtown apartments because he did not want Barbara following him to the home he shared with Lacy.

§§§

Marilyn left threatening messages on his private cell phone when she realized that she was taking the fall alone. The money she gave Alexander made her want him to take the fall with her, but she had no proof to tie him to any of her illegal dealings. Now Brown Foster was being investigated by the SEC and on the verge of bankruptcy. She tried conspiring with Mr. Brown to involve Alexander, only to learn he couldn't because he had personally signed-off on the underhanded deals. Alexander's signature couldn't be found on one single document and, thanks to Shonna, now he had some incriminating information on Mr. Brown that guaranteed his silence.

§§§

Alexander confidently walked into Mr. Brown office, gripping his briefcase at his side. "So, what's up, Geoff? You wanted to see me?"

Geoff looked up from the stack of papers scattered on his desk. "You know we're in deep shit, right?"

"Yes, I do. What do you want me to do about it?"

"Well, someone is going to have to take the fall for it and you benefited well. I thought you would step up, but since you haven't, I'm going to make sure everyone knows your involvement in this. They all will be pointing the finger at you."

Alexander pointed a finger toward himself. "At me, I don't think so. Why, because I was the only black guy in the room? Geoff, you got me fucked up. If you go back through all of the documents, you won't find my name on shit. I knew this would happen, but guess what? I'm not the dumbest guy in the room, Geoff. That would be you!" Alexander opened his briefcase and pulled out a video and pictures of Geoff chained up while two black men pleasured him. He also had pictures of him faced down in a mound of cocaine. He threw the pictures on Geoff's desk. "You can have this set because I have plenty more. By the way, what do you think your wife and children would say about this?"

He turned around and walked out, leaving Geoff screaming. "What the fuck is this? Where did you get these?"

Alexander knew he had Geoff by the balls.

"You're going to pay, Al, I promise you. If it's the last thing I do, you will pay."

CHAPTER SEVEN

Lacy's cell phone rang and she grabbed it from her purse. "Hello!"

"Ms. Williams?"

"Yes, this is she."

"Ms. Williams, this Officer Gilbert Jones."

"Yes?"

"You called earlier and reported your boyfriend shot and lying in a pool of blood in your home?"

"Yes, yes I did."

"Well Ms. is this some kind of joke you're pulling because we're over at your place now and there is no body, no blood, nothing! Do you know filing a false police report is a serious crime and you could go to jail for this?"

"What? Look sir, I'm not lying. I heard the gunshots. I saw his body. He was there. And so was the shooter. I heard him coming after me."

"Do you know what the perpetrator looks like?"

"No, I never saw him. I could only hear him coming; I took off running and never looked back."

"Since you are so adamant about what you saw, we would like to bring you in for questioning. There is an officer in front of your sister's house now."

"Why? Instead of badgering me you need to figure out what happened to Alexander."

"Just go with the officer, Ms. Williams. We intend to get this all straightened out."

Chapter Eight

Alexander lay near the basement door of the home where Lacy and he has spent three years together. Quiet tears filled his eyes as he reminisced over the last three years of his life. He had done some ruthless things to some good people, especially Lacy. He felt his behavior toward her had been brutal and callous.

Once he realized she was long gone, he rose from the floor. He removed the blood bag, cleaned up the blood from the floor. Then, he quickly showered, grabbed his coat and exited the house from the rear. A black 2011 Crown Victoria, with tinted windows waited for him. He hopped in the back seat and they drove off.

The driver handed Alexander a small black briefcase. "Nice job Robert, your mission was successful. You have provided us with enough information to take down Brown Foster and your snow bonnie, Marilyn, for embezzling money from the bank. We got the extra bonus of putting an end to their secret prostitution ring. There are agents on their way to pick everyone up."

Robert had been an undercover agent for twelve years. He wished he could enjoy the feeling of accomplishment, but this assignment had changed him. He had become a monster. It was okay being hardcore with men, but never in his career had he treated a woman the way he treated Lacy. "What about Lacy, what will happen to her?"

"Lacy will be fine, Robert. Now don't go soft on me now. The officer will question her, but eventually she will be let go. She will be able to utilize the investments you set up in her name. Lacy will be fine."

Robert sat in the back seat with his head hung low. "I just want to be sure she will be okay."

"She was just part of the con. You started out playing her, but you fell in love with her, didn't you?"

Robert never responded.

SA'RAI
LM BLAKELY

CHAPTER ONE

I'm lying here naked...sodomized, raped, bludgeoned and coming down from a heroin binge with no fight left in me. Just before I took my last breath three hours ago, I could still hear their voices lingering in the background of the church disguised as one of the highest, one of the adorned and highly favored. Both men, ashamed of their infidelity, were fueled by the power they had over me. Their breath was hot, poisoned by the Jack Daniels that they faithfully, yet secretly, drank from their flask. Who would've ever thought the church where my mother abandoned me on that cold night, the day after Christmas, would be the place I took my last breath?

My life has been far from perfect. From the beginning, my birth mother left me in a basket on the church steps, nameless and swaddled in a red blanket. She had pinned a note to it stating that I was born on Christmas day, but her father forced her to give me away. Unfortunately, my grandfather happens to also be my father, which also makes my mother my sister. One of the nuns, Mother Anna Crystal found me on the doorstep and named me Sa'rai, pronounced Sa-Rye.

Mother AC raised me as if I was her own child. She carried me in her heart, since she never wed and birthed any children of her own. She saw to it that I was schooled amongst the other children in the church and made sure there was never a possibility for me being adopted. When I turned thirteen, several different priests started requesting me to come in their study to clean and organize their bookcases, which later led to them forcing sex upon me. Sworn to secrecy, I could never repeat to anyone the acts that were taking place, not even when I became pregnant at the age of sixteen. One of the priests requested my services every day and silently it became a battle amongst the priests until I became his territory. Mother AC kicked me out when she learned the news. Without a clue of how to survive in the streets of New York, I was forced into an unfamiliar life.

Lost and pregnant, I no longer had someone spying over my shoulder, calculating my every move. My freedom was now at my fingertips. Saddened that the priests violated my body and denied fathering my unborn child, I no longer believed in the Word as I once had. I became rebellious and started selling my body for money. Why should I treasure what the priests so lustfully violated?

Who would've thought that ten years later I would be here? I wasn't on the streets like majority of the women I met and competed against. I preferred rich businessmen, entrepreneurs, government officials, priests and professional athletes. I wanted their money and in return they wanted companionship and I gave them exactly what they paid for. Nothing was left untouched, not even conversation. I could be whatever they wanted. My occupation afforded me a luxurious lifestyle and I made sure my son, David, reaped the benefits of it by attending one of the best Catholic schools money could buy. Life was good, but I had a secret. I was addicted to something, an awful habit I picked up so my conscience wouldn't wear me down. Heroin, but I called it *Passion*. And no matter how much I tried to leave it alone, the high always enticed me. The high has always trickled down my spine, landing in between my legs, leaving me alone as I pulsated, clinching to the thought of someone touching or caressing me with immense sexual hunger without it costing him a dime. One of the curses of this industry always had me longing for a real relationship. Still, I was chasing the high and the money and as a result, it always forced me to choose it to pay my bills.

CHAPTER TWO

Three days before Christmas Eve, I received a service request from an anonymous companion while I was with another client. Initially I declined the request, hoping to spend some time my son, but I accepted the offer when I learned how much he was willing to pay. The amount he proposed could buy my son and me a one-way ticket out of New York so we could start anew.

When the day finally arrived, I stepped in the dimly lit hotel room, second guessing myself. That was the first time I didn't trust a situation in a long time, but when I glanced over towards him to decline his offer, he seemed anxious, half-naked and heavily intoxicated from what looked like a Jack Daniels Tennessee Whiskey bottle that sat on the night stand. When I saw what he was drinking, I immediately recognized who he was. I turned around just as he was walking towards me, bruising my neck with his stained breath.

"What are you doing here?" I asked, almost in a whisper.

"Do you really need to ask that?" he said with slurred speech as his fingers traced the top of my shoulders.

"I don't want your money..." I said as I walked away from him.

"Wait...I'm lonely," he said when he grabbed my hand. "Christmas is days away and my wife has been sick for months. She won't even look at me, let alone touch me," he said in a softer voice.

I sighed reluctantly. I did not want any part of this night. The thought of him touching me sickened me and I didn't want to participate.

"I need to decline your offer," I said without looking at him.

"Please, I have money. I will pay you double."

I closed my eyes, took a deep breath and bit my bottom lip.

"I need the money upfront," I said with a stare when I turned to look at him.

"I have it," he said in a rushed tone as he shoved the two stacks of one hundred dollar bills into my hands. "Wait, I have more," he said as he ran towards the closet. His desperate act made me think back to when I was under his care as a child. The pain never healed and allowing him to pay me for sex only triggered old wounds.

When he emptied his bag of money on the bed, the look in his eyes was cold and distant. He only cared about his needs, unconcerned about whom he violated. I knew he didn't recognize me when he looked at me, so there was no use in exchanging useless banter. I never made sex personal nor did I reveal my true identity to anyone. My clients called me "Passion." I was their drug as heroin was mine. The child I bore at sixteen came from the man that stood no more than two steps away from me. His only reason for coming here was for sexual favors, nothing more. I'm sure if the church knew he was swindling money from them for sex, he would be defrocked from priesthood.

I went to the restroom, wrapped my rubber tube around my arm and injected a double dose into my veins. I smiled to myself for a second while it traveled its way through my veins straight to my loins. I took my shower, splashed myself with some perfume and then returned to the room as the high took over my body. I grabbed my phone and took pictures of us for insurance, just in case he tried to become problematic afterwards. Sometimes men thought you belonged to them after they spent you money for sex. After a night of rushed, uneventful intercourse, I looked at him once more before I stuffed the cash in my purse and left him drunk and chained to the bed.

Chapter Three

I picked David up from a friend's house and went home only to find an eviction notice on my door. I ripped it off and went in to find my mail strewn across the hall floor. Honestly, looking at the mail made me realized I hadn't been home in almost a week. David had been staying at my neighbors because I told them I had a potential job opportunity in Detroit. Flipping through the junk mail and envelopes, I noticed a letter from my son's school and quickly opened it only to read that my account was three months delinquent. I grabbed all the mail and stuffed it in my purse before we walked back towards the car. I wasn't sure where we were going, but I had enough money for us to start a brand new life outside of New York.

"Mommy, it's cold out here," David said with a shudder. "And I'm hungry."

Still high on my binge, food was the last thing I wanted, but whatever David wanted, he got.

"I know," I said as I drove to Lombardi's Pizza.

We stepped away from the car, entered the establishment and ordered our pizza. David asked that we sit down and eat since he hadn't seen me for almost a week. He had insisted that I cook him a full meal before I mentioned pizza, his favorite. My high was coming down, but I needed to think of a plan for us. I looked through my purse and pulled out the mail before our breadsticks arrived and noticed a letter from the health department. I opened it while David talked about baseball tryouts in the spring and read what it disclosed. I looked at him, then back at the words on the letter. My eyes slipped away from the paper towards the window and I noticed a tow truck towing my car away from the restaurant.

"Hey, asshole!" I screamed and jumped up from the table.

My legs were numb from the double dose I'd taken hours ago. My feet wouldn't allow me to run after my car, but I tried to walk as fast as I could.

"Damn it!" I screamed when the tow truck turned the corner.

I dropped my head. Today's events totally frustrated me. David began to ask twenty-one questions and that added to my aggravation.

"Now how are we gonna get home?" he asked.

"David, sit down and eat," I said calmly, disguising my annoyance.

"But Mom..."

"David, sit your ass down and eat your damn food."

I needed a break from everything. At times, I wish I had an aunt, uncle or cousins I could call. Hell, at this point, I just wanted a friend who would watch over David until I worked this out.

"What are you going to do about the car?" David said.

I sighed.

"I'll be right back; I'm going to the restroom. Eat your food and don't move."

I walked away from him, swiftly, hoping no one was occupying the restroom. When I stepped inside of it, I ran into a stall, locked the door, pulled out my kit, took the tube and tied it around my arm as tight as I could. I reached into my purse, got the syringe and thumped it. My lips quivered from the thought of the high I was about to inject into my body, but more so, the thought of the high aroused me. I carefully shot myself with another dose of Passion, placed it back in my purse and leaned back on the toilet as I escaped the troubles I was now facing.

Damn, no car, no home and now AIDS?

I looked in my purse to see how much Passion was left and realized it wasn't enough for another hit. It didn't matter how life or people failed me, Passion was always there to comfort me. It never betrayed me, never left me lonely, never made me cry and it never broke my heart like everyone I had ever met. I didn't want to face this reality. Leaving David was never an option, but now...I had to make sure David was going to have a better life than I did. I couldn't cry yet, I had too much to do. I opened the stall, walked towards the sink and splashed some cold water on my face.

Something was wrong. I'm not claiming AIDS. I know damn well I went to the doctor months ago and my test results were still negative. Well, actually...who am I fooling?

CHAPTER FOUR

Nine years ago, after I initially went to the doctor to get tested, he called me to come in for the results. I was furious when he said it was positive and demanded a retest. He told me it was perfectly normal for me to be upset, but did the re-test for my peace of mind. Shockingly, the results came back negative. He couldn't explain the mishap and he told me to make sure I came back every month for re-testing. When he saw the bruises on my arm, he knew I was using. He offered to help me with several programs, but I wasn't interested, so he handed me a month supply of clean needles and warned me never to share. If I returned the used ones to him, he would dispose of them. To date, he always tried to give me brochures on centers and programs, but I declined them. The last time I went to see him, he said he would be relocating to another office somewhere out west. I took my HIV test and he jotted down his new number on his business card and gave it to me just before I left his office.

My mind raced back to the letter. I'm sure somebody made a mistake. I grabbed my purse, pushed my hair away from my face and took a long, deep breath. I walked back towards my son and sat in front of him with glazed eyes, a throbbing crotch and feeling sick to my stomach from the aroma of the food sitting directly in front of me.

"Figured you wanted your usual 7-UP," David said without looking at me.

"Thank you," I answered, almost ashamed.

For a second, I wondered if he knew I used. I wondered if he knew all my secrets. David never questioned me. He just took control and took care of me without a single complaint.

"Mommy, can I ask you something?"

I looked at him, slightly nervous about the questions on the tip of his tongue. I wiped my forehead with a napkin as he spoke.

"Where are we going with no car? No place to stay? A shelter? Church?" he asked with a straight face.

"I will get the car back, don't worry about that. As far as us going somewhere, I'm not sure...I need to make some phone calls," I said in my calmest voice.

"Oh, I forgot to tell you, the other day a woman came by the house when I was outside playing with Rashad..."

"What woman?"

"I don't know. She looked kinda like you..."

I looked away. I wasn't sure who knew where I stayed. I kept to myself so friends were something I didn't really have...just clients.

"Did she leave her name? A number? Message?"

"No, oh, wait a minute," he said as he pulled out an envelope. "She did tell me to give you this."

He handed me a sealed envelope.

"Why didn't you open it?"

"You want me to?"

"Sure, go 'head."

With excitement, he threw his fork down, ripped the envelope open and pulled out a folded piece of paper. He looked at her and cleared his throat while he unfolded the letter.

> Hi,
> I hope this letter find you in good spirits. My name is Mila Royal. Twenty six years ago, I had a baby and brought her to the doorsteps of church miles away from where I stayed. Scared and threatened by my father, I had no choice but to leave her in a basket covered with my favorite red

blanket. I've always thought of her and wanted to find her. Five years after I had her, I came back to the church, but no one knew what I was talking about. They claimed there hadn't been a baby left on their doorstep. Confused, I left because I didn't know where to go from there. Six weeks ago, I went back to the church hoping to speak to someone who had worked there that dreadful night, but no one could help me.

As I was leaving, I ran into this pudgy guy. He spoke to me as if he knew my heart and my intentions, although he spoke in riddles. Later I found out it was a scripture from the Bible. I read the scripture, hoping there was a message in it for me, but I couldn't find one. Then one day while I was journaling, I realized that I read it twice a day to my puppy Goliath. After we returned from the park, I had a vision of 211 Park Place and I took a drive to the address. I wasn't sure where Park Place was or why I should drive over there. The first time I arrived, I wasn't sure who lived there but then I saw your son and I knew God sent me to the right place. You and your son are a spitting image of me and on a whim; I just took this chance to write this letter. I've enclosed my business card with my phone numbers for you. I would love to talk.

Always, Mila.

I sat in silence, unsure if I had heard correctly or if he had read the letter right.

"Who is Mila?" he asked.

"I'm not sure. Make sure you put that card in your pocket, we may need to call her later."

"Okay."

I reached for my phone and dialed the number I'd committed to memory whenever I was low on my stash. In less than five seconds, he picked up, acknowledged my call and asked for my location.

Since he's coming this way, maybe he can drop us off at the church.

I asked the server to pack up the remnants of our pizza and then paid for our meal. David looked at me, his head tilted to the right as if he wanted to ask me something, but he never said a word. I could only imagine what was going through his mind and Lord knows my mind was all over the place. When I saw my connection pull up outside, I told David to wait with our food and adjusted my coat and scarf to keep the snow off me as I walked outside towards his car. He rolled down the window as I approached.

"Will you take me and David to the church?"

"The church? That's why you hit me up?"

"No," I said, throwing him a three crispy hundred dollar bills.

"Get in," he said, rolling up his window.

I turned around and waved for David to come to the car. I jumped into the passenger seat and quickly stuffed my package in my purse.

"You got enough to hold you down for the holidays?"

"Y-yes."

"Look, Sa'rai, I know I sound biased, but how many times do I have to tell you that you're too beautiful to be pumping your veins with his shit? You're a functional addict and I don't want to be a part of your habit when the New Year comes."

"When did you decide this?"

"I've been beating myself up about this. I don't want anything to happen to you and I don't want it to be because I've been enabling you."

"Every time I try to stop, it...calls...me...back," she said in a low whisper while looking at her hands.

"What about..." he started to ask when the backdoor flew open.

"Hey, Uncle Snap."

"What's good, son? You keepin' them grades up?"

"Yes, sir. I have to if I'm going to play basketball."

"You any good? What position you trying to play?"

"Point."

I couldn't believe they were having such a normal conversation while I was secretly dealing with my own shit storm. I closed my eyes, trying to hold back the tears that welled in my eyes, but I dare not drop a tear, not in front of my son. I tuned them out until I felt Snap's hand on my thigh.

"You sure you want to go back there?" Snap directed his question to me.

"I need to take care of some business before I figure out what we are going to do. I've mishandled my finances and my car was towed. I can't do anything until after the holidays."

"You guys can come to my place 'til you figure things out. As far as your car, don't worry about it. Just hit me up when you're done, I'll come back and get you two and we will get your car out today."

"Thank you."

"No problem."

Snap pulled up to the church, avoiding the mounds of snow piled up at the curb with ease.

"Alright, lil man, I'll catch up with you later."

I waved at Snap as he pulled off and turned around to face the church I had left years ago. Silently I took a deep breath. I quickly said a prayer for strength before I opened the large church doors and looked around for anyone.

"May I help you?" a young man asked politely.

"Um, yes...I would like to go to the confessionals."

"Let me see if someone is still here. I know the priests were trying to leave."

I looked away and shifted my weight to one side.

"Is Mother AC, or Mother Anna Crystal here?"

Saying that name brought back chills. She was the only mother I knew. I had new questions about Mila Royal and I needed answers. *Who was she? Where did she come from? Who sent her?*

"Give me a second, please have a seat," the young gentleman said as he disappeared from the dimly lit cathedral.

"Mommy, who is Mother Anna Crystal?" David whispered.

"She is...a..." I tried to figure out a way to explain who she was and was grateful when the young man returned quietly. His mannerisms brought back old memories of when I was younger. I wondered if the priests were still carrying out their sinful acts of lust on the children who were still there.

"Ma'am, please follow me."

We followed the young man and I could tell that David was amazed by the church from the way he kept looking around. I never took him to church. Engulfed in my own thoughts, I wasn't paying attention to what our guide was saying until we stopped walking.

"Here you go, have a merry Christmas and a happy new year," he finally said with a smile.

"You too."

I tapped on the door lightly, just like she requested when I lived here.

"Come in," she said.

I instantly recognized her voice. It made me shudder, but while I stared at her, I stood, speechless and frozen in my stance. David waited beside me, but must have noticed my resistance because he grabbed my hand as if to reassure me that everything would be okay.

"Hello, Sa'rai," she said, removing her horn-rimmed glasses from her face.

"Mother, I need to talk to you."

"Dear Lord," she gasped. "What a beautiful woman you turned out to be," Mother Anna said as she welcomed them in.

"Thank you."

"Please, have a seat," she said, pointing towards the matching chairs in front of her desk. "I've missed you."

I didn't know how to respond and a sigh escaped my lips. David looked confused, but somehow knew better than to pry with his questions at that moment.

"Would you like to go somewhere and talk?"

"I need to go to the confessionals, but we can talk here until someone is available."

"Um, most of the priests are leaving for the holidays, but there is one available tonight. Let me see if there is someone who will sit with you and hear your confession."

"Thank you."

After she placed the phone back into its cradle, she walked around her desk and leaned her bottom against it.

"So, who might this young man be?"

I paused at her question. At that moment, I was unsure if I wanted her to know anything about us. Clearly, I was a mess, but if anyone should know me, it would be Mother Anna. I slowly cleared my throat and smiled at my pride and joy.

"This is my son, David."

"David? Yes, David and Goliath used to be one of your favorite stories," Mother said with a faint smile.

David looked even more confused. I placed my hand on his knee and told him I would explain later. He nodded reluctantly. I knew my reason for wanting to speak to Mother Anna so I got straight to the point.

"David, do you still have the letter?"

"Yes." He took the envelope from his pocket and gave it to me.

"Mother, could you please explain this?" I said when I handed her the letter, leaving Mila's business card in the envelope.

Mother grabbed the letter, placed her glasses back on and gasped as she read the letter. She put the letter down and looked at me, hiding her expression. I tried to read her face, but to no avail.

"Is Mila Royal the person she says she is to me?" I asked.

Mother AC turned around slightly, as if trying to ignore my question.

"Mother AC, I need to know...if she is my...mother."

Before she could answer, the gentleman who escorted us to Mother Anna tapped on her door.

"I found a couple of Fathers who haven't left yet. One is available for your confession."

"Thank you," I said. I immediately glanced at her, hoping she would answer me. "We need to finish this, I won't be long."

I stood up, kissed the top of David's head and whispered in his ear.

"Trust no one but her."

"Yes, she is, Sa'Rai," she blurted out once I reached the door.

I stopped mid-stride before turning to look at her. I nodded my head in agreement and then stared at David. My heart raced. I wasn't sure how I felt but, at that moment, both an uneasiness and relief came over me. Before I knew it, a tear fell. I followed the gentleman and he led me to the confessional. I stepped into the familiar booth, closed the door behind me and nervously sat down, blindly searching my purse until my fingers ran across my kit with the stash Snap gave me earlier.

"Are you there?" I whispered as I pulled out my phone.

I took Mila's card from the envelope and sent her a text message. When I called out for the priest again, no one answered. I quickly wrapped my tubing around my wrist and placed the needle into the first raised vein I saw in my hand. I injected the very small dosage slowly, getting an immediate rush while a priest sat beside me with the wall separating us. He started his prayer. I heard a thud nearby and instantly became paranoid, quickly pulling the needle out as Passion aroused me.

"Forgive me Father for I have sinned. I've lived with burdens that I no longer wish to carry..."

As I began my prayer, it felt like a weight lifted and my problems weren't as heavy as they once were. My heart didn't feel the pain of the heartbreaking stories I lived my entire life. It was difficult, almost too much to bear. I had no family except for Mother AC, the priests sexually assaulted me, I became pregnant and then after disclosing my pregnancy, they threw me into the streets of New York. And it didn't stop there. Unprepared for the hatred in the world, I felt lost to the streets and with a son, I had to make sure money was coming in the best way I knew how. I tried to go to school to get my high school diploma, but failed. My relationships failed, too. The only thing that brought me through it all was Passion, introduced to me by a client. Regardless of what the outcome would be, allowing my burdens to pour from my mouth to his ears relieved me of my haunted past. The priest didn't utter a sound when I revealed the names of the men who secretly ravished my innocence for their predatory appetite.

CHAPTER FIVE

The confessional that was once warm grew cold as if we were suddenly outside in the winter air. I shuddered in silence. *Was I alone in the booth?* I leaned over and waited to hear him breathe, but my intuition told me the priest was gone.

When I reached down to grab my purse, I became dizzy. My head was spinning from my last injection. Suddenly, I felt a blow to my head and the prick of a needle in my neck. Before I could lift my head, someone snatched my arms from under me and dragged me out of the confessional towards a dark room. I had no idea where they were taking me, but I heard familiar voices. I tried to yell, scream and kick, but they covered my mouth and held my wrists tightly.

As they held me with my face down, I tried my best to get a glimpse of them, but found I was unable to turn my head. I felt numb, but a cool breeze indicated my clothes were being ripped from my body. Paralyzed by the drug and the men who held me against my will, it was as if I knew the script by heart. I actually expected them to violate me all over again.

"I thought he told you to stay away from here? We know you chained Father Dunklin to the bed and we will carry out your punishment. You had to come back and run your mouth, eh?" one of the priests said as his breath brushed my right earlobe, making me aware that he was having his way with me again. For some reason I couldn't feel a thing in my loins. He repositioned himself and began to sodomize me as he quietly chastised me. I heard another voice tell him to hurry up because he also wanted to re-teach me a lesson. When he climbed on me, it was hard for me to breathe. Something was terribly wrong because I heard a loud banging noise and saw blood pooling around me. The second priest thrust himself against my backside, literally tearing my flesh. I heard him stand up and collect himself as the two talked amongst themselves as if I wasn't there; naked...sodomized, raped and bludgeoned. They splashed something on me and spoke in Latin. I assumed it was holy water, but it smelled something like bleach.

At that moment, I had no fight left. I couldn't fight for my son who was there, unaware of what was happening to me and I am at least thankful for that. As I closed my eyes for what felt like the last time, I could hear the priests arguing about who should stay the night until they abruptly stopped. They finally left the room and closed the door behind them. I heard someone humming and popping their fingers to the beat of their own drum and weakly opened my eyes when I heard the door open, but a cloud of comforting peace fell upon me as the person walked in. I then fell into my last sleep.

CHAPTER SIX

Iam approached the priests and inarguably offered to stay during the holidays while they went home to be with their loved ones. No questions were asked and no one cared to stick around longer to walk through the church with Iam. As he whistled throughout the church, something called him to one of the confessionals. Before entering, he stopped as if he knew someone was in need on the other side of the door. Just as he turned the knob to walk in, he opened his hands and covered the room with peace and deliverance. He didn't judge anyone for their actions or their decisions or the situations we faced. Instead, he focused on the purity in their hearts. Just hours earlier, the woman who laid in her own blood in front of him had humbly begged for HIS forgiveness for her sins. She was now forgiven. He looked at her, noticing what her accusers have done to her and shook his head in dismay. He saw the hammer underneath the chair and the nails scattered around the floor. They had pierced her hands and feet to the hardwood floor in front of him. Iam forcefully removed the nails from her hands and feet with his hands, picked her up leaving her clothes scattered on the floor behind them and slowly carried her towards a table. He covered her with a white cloth, walked towards Mother Anna Crystal's door and opened it. Mother AC was telling David who Mila Royal was and how she knew his mother. She looked up, grabbed David's hand and placed him behind her when the door flung open.

"Hello?" Mother Anna said towards the unoccupied door.

Her pause seemed to last forever. She took a deep breath and walked towards the door to see who opened it, but no one stood there. She could feel the faint cool air that seemingly led the way to another location. Holding onto David's hand, Mother AC followed the breeze until she came to a chilly room that was used for Bible study. When she looked in, she could see something on the table draped with a white cloth, but she was hesitant to see who was underneath.

She tried to block David's view, but he was curious to see who or what was underneath the sheet as well. Mother Anna lifted the sheet just enough to view what was under it, but hurriedly dropped it when she saw Sa'Rai's face. She gasped, closed her eyes and held her head down as her grip on David's hand tightened. Mother AC took a deep breath and tried to usher him out of the classroom before he could see, but it was too late. A bloody hand dropped off the table from under the sheet and he froze when he saw his mother's ring.

"Mommy?" he asked with uncertainty in his voice.

Mother AC tightly wrapped her arms around him and brought him closer to her body just as Mila walked into the sanctuary. She stepped closer to the woman and child. Mother AC gasps as she came face to face with the woman. *Dear God, she looks like an older version of Sa'rai!* David lifted his head and stared into Mila's eyes.

"My name's Mila Royal and I got a text message to come here. I'm looking for Mother Anna Crystal?" Mila asked.

"I'm Mother Anna Crystal."

"I tried calling the number I received the message from, but no one picked up. Is everything ok?"

Mother Anna looked away and stepped aside, revealing the covered body behind her. Mila, unsure what to say or do, looked at David.

"Are you okay?" she asked.

He wiped his eyes, noticing the woman's familiar face.

"I'm ..."

"My grandmother?" he asked.

"Yes."

Silently, David walked towards his mother's body. Although young, he knew she had an addiction and always dreaded the day he would lose her to drugs. He'd even heard his best friend's parents argue about it when they thought he was asleep. David held his head down and hesitantly pulled the covers away from his mother's face. Mila was astounded to see what he uncovered and rushed to take him away, but he stood beside his mother, longing to hear her voice once more, to feel her wrap her arms around him just one last time. A part of him wanted to scream, but the growing anger brewing inside him began to pump through his veins. David grabbed her wounded hand and slowly pulled the bloody ring off her finger, the same ring Snap had given her six months ago. He always said he was going to save her from herself and make her his wife. He often said he would give up everything to be with her. She always laughed, but David knew Snap really meant it. David put the ring in his pocket and placed her hand back on the table before Mila pulled the sheet back up over her face. She gently wrapped her arm around David and turned him toward the church exit. Just as they walked past Mother AC, she reached her hand towards Mila, hoping to stop them. Mila asked David to sit down in the last pew so she could talk with Mother Anna for a quick second. He walked away and did as he was told. Mila then turned to talk to Mother Anna as soon as David was out of earshot.

"I'm sure Sa'Rai texted you..." Mother AC said with a teary pause. "She probably wants David with you."

"He is my grandson, so rightfully he should come with me," Mila said.

"How do know you he's your grandson? Has he been tested? He can stay here until the test is done. He's no bother; he will fit right in here with the other kids."

"No bother? Someone just murdered my daughter in this church, but all you can say is that he's no bother ..."

"What are you insinuating?"

"I'm not insinuating anything; I'm just stating the facts. How about I take him with me? I will bring him back so you can see him. I will also bring the DNA results back with me," Mila advised. "Is that a problem?"

Mother Anna looked around and then softly whispered, "No..."

"Has anyone called the police?"

"I'm not certain," Mother Anna said.

Mila pulled out her phone to dial 911 and talked to the dispatcher while Mother Anna mumbled to herself. After she hung up, she waited with David for the police to arrive. David sat in the back, watching everyone and pulled out the cell phone his mother bought him. He sent Snap a text telling him to come to the church. David closed his eyes and rested his head on the back of the pew while he waited for Snap to reply.

"Young man," Iam said as he came to sit beside David. "I'm sure you have unanswered questions about what just happened. Nothing is ever too hard for you to handle despite the consequences, trials and tribulations you're faced with right now. Just remember you are not alone and that is why Mila is here. Trust her. Her intentions are good. Her love is deep. Go with her; take your mother's life with you so you can be the man you are destined to become. Your mother's life was not in vain if you follow the right path."

"Yeah, it just seems so unfair," he said without opening his swollen eyes.

"Right now, it might seem unfair, but she's in a much better place, a more peaceful place. She doesn't have to worry about anything anymore or carry her burdens any longer. Now it's time for you to learn that love exists beyond the pain that you're experiencing."

David lifted his head and opened his eyes to look at the person he was talking to, but no one was there. He quickly looked around, breathing as fast as his racing heart. He stood up and walked towards his grandmother with an almost angelic look on his face.

"What's wrong, David?" Mila asked as he ran into her embrace.

With an overwhelming calming embrace, she held onto David as he silently cried. Once the police arrived, she watched as the three officers spoke to Mother Anna while the coroner removed Sa'Rai's body from the church. Mila looked at David once more.

"What's wrong, David?" she asked again.

"I think I just had a conversation with God."

STATE STREET
JA GARDNER

Reverends George and Louis had been arguing for hours when the main doors banged open against the walls and a pudgy man walked in snapping and popping his fingers.

"May we help you?" They spoke, not quite in unison, but with the same questioning tone.

"Yes, I guess you can or perhaps I can help you."

"What is it that you need?"

Reverend Louis' voice sounded tired. He and Reverend George had been bickering on and off for days and his patience was running thin.

"Let me introduce myself. The name's Iam G. and I believe I can help you with your dilemma."

Reverend George's response quickly moved from ministering to annoyed. He wanted to get home to his family and now this guy shows up selling something. If it wasn't Reverend Louis and his whining, it seemed it was going to be the oddly-dressed salesman who worked on his last nerve.

Iam wore a dark brown plaid suit with a belt the size of a cummerbund. His shoes were black and buffed to a glowing shine.

The church often brought in strangers from all over the world. In fact, the entire Portsborough community was filled with landmark status homes bringing tourist, students and historians all the time.

It was just this status that made everything so difficult. There were so many changes to implement with so little funding. The community was suffering a bit after several recent burglaries and Community Affairs, along with the church board, were working hard to close and lock the doors after the last service of the day. Reverend George didn't agree with the board or Louis but, against his better judgment, he was afraid they would close them anyway.

"How did you get in?" Reverend George asked Iam and threw an accusing look at Reverend Louis. "You didn't lock the doors, did you?" Iam thought they would be back to arguing in a minute if he didn't step in.

"Louis, I believe we have another problem at the moment," George declared and turned back to Iam. "I'm certain you *cannot* help us."

"No, I can. I can take over for the night and you can go home to your families."

"You most certainly cannot." The look of horror on both their faces showed Iam they could at least agree on something.

"Please sit for a moment. I'm sure, after thinking this over, you'll see that I can."

They looked to the Chancel and murmured quietly, lips moving rapidly, presumably in prayer. Each glanced one additional time at Iam before speaking to each other again.

"Thank you. Had you asked me if I would permit this just a few hours ago, I would have said no. But it feels like the right thing to do."

George's reluctance was still there and for a moment Iam wasn't certain the priests would go home to their families.

Having the church to himself always felt good. He would much rather sit and enjoy the quiet, but there was much work to be done.

§§§

She smelled like jasmine when she walked up to the chick in front of me and flashed a smile to step ahead in line. The chick stepped back and landed on my toe while trying to let her pass. I would've said something if the jasmine-smelling one hadn't been so pretty.

When I stepped out of the store, they were talking by the car. It looked like there was some trouble with the lock. Maybe this was my lucky day. I could sure use some. I was about to offer to help when I overheard their conversation.

"Sometimes, if you jiggle it…"

The jasmine-smelling one looked up with a sexy smile, "Yeah, tried that. Jiggle this way, that way, slide it in but not too far."

I recognized the laughter that followed. It was the kind you hear when someone's sharing a private joke that everyone, but you, knows. Bad enough the world had gone mad and told these people they could live together like they were real couples, but listening to them, talk about it just fucked me up.

I turned around after deciding to head back and catch up with Z. He said he had something for me. Just before the light changed, I heard Jasmine, as I'd called her in my mind, say her name. Chaun. Damn, she even has a guy name. Fucked up, anyway you look at it.

§§§

"Thanks for helping me with the lock. My name's Chaun, Chaun King by the way."

"Tracy Charters. Is that Atlanta I hear or perhaps a place further southwest?" Tracy asked.

"It's Georgia for sure, Augusta to be specific. Spent most of my life there and then decided a few years ago to see what New York was all about. You're the first person to get it right in a long time. Most people immediately say Texas or Florida. What about you, New Yorker, right?"

"Through and through and I'm an excellent tour guide for newbies."

"I'm not new." She smiled as she answered. "I've been here almost two years." We conversed while leaning against the car, the lock forgotten. "I could go for some tea right now. If you have time, we could continue our conversation at that diner on Cadman?"

§§§

We hit it off right away. We talked for a long time over breakfast. By the time we walked back to my car, I was hoping to see Tracy again in the near future. She'd listened to my story about being a photographer and how I was working on a visual storytelling project with my parents as the main focus, how I'd come from a happy home and wanted the world to know about it, but I wanted to know more about her.

§§§

"Last week when I was in North Carolina, a friend of a friend stopped by with some new tools he'd picked up. You mentioned a need so I picked something up for you. Check 'em out. I gotta hit the head."

"Tools? You came here to show me tools? That's not what we talked about." Cisco's mood was bad. Things were sliding down hill for him pretty damn fast. His friends had stopped listening to him complain. He thought that maybe it was the one room living arrangement that added to his stress. *How much longer could it last?*

"Just look in the bag, man."

"You know you get on my nerves. Seems like every damn day for the past five years, even when I ask for just one thing, you still fucking bring me..."

"Like I said, I thought you could use it." Z came out of the bathroom and stood right behind him, admiring the gun he had picked up for him. It was a small black anodized 9mm designed for concealment. It was light in weight, but deadly in the long-run.

"Might even fit in that empty holster you been carrying around for the last few years."

§§§

My apartment on State Street is a garden apartment without a garden. Still I loved it and couldn't wait until Chaun came by for dinner. Though we'd only just met yesterday, the breakfast, the conversation, the laughter, all went so well that I found myself thinking about asking her to dinner before I walked her back to her car.

The weather was unseasonably warm, so I thought I grill some Portobello mushrooms on the outdoor grill the landlord installed and framed with granite cooking tiles. He was a do-it-yourselfer and I was reaping the benefits. I was just about to put the salad in the fridge to cool and uncork a bottle of merlot when the doorbell rang. I rushed to it like a teenager on a first date, all butterflies and butter fingers.

"Let me get your coat and give you the tour." In my best tour guide voice, I said, "It isn't very long, but if you get thirsty there's wine here in the kitchen to go with the dinner, a working fireplace that should just be heating up and down that very short hallway is the bathroom on the left and my bedroom on the right. Make yourself at home. I have to check the grill."

"Can we eat by a fire or would you be too warm for that?"

"I guess it is chilly for a southerner." I poked fun at her just a bit and hoped she would be okay with it.

"Forty-five degrees is not chilly. It's cold even for you Northerners." Only when she said it her accent made it sound more like *northenuh*. I liked her answer.

"If you're not up for the red on the counter," I called from the grill. "There are other reds in the wine cabinet. The white wine is there in the wine fridge below the counter."

"Red's fine and what smells so good?"

I looked up to see she was at the back door, shoes off, but wearing my hoodie. She really had made herself at home.

"Grilled Portobellos and I sliced fresh mozzarella too, if you like cheese."

"You're quite the cliché!" Her dreadlocks were bouncing as she laughed and looked for the wine glasses.

"Second shelf on the left and why am I a cliché?"

"Vegetarian. Lesbian. It's a fairly well-circulated rumor, you know."

"Not a vegetarian, just didn't know if you were or not."

"So we could have had some grilled pork chops? Good to know." I hated to think of her as sassy because it did seem like a stereotype, her being from the South and all, but sassy seemed to fit what looked to be about one hundred and forty pounds of beautiful brown-skinned woman. Her locks were a kind of rusty color that gave her a glow.

Chaun was opening and closing cabinet doors looking for plates while I stoked the fire and turned the mushrooms.

With the garden doors closed, I didn't have to raise my voice for her to hear me. "Tell me more about your visual story. What makes it so interesting?"

"My parents were born in Augusta, but lived in New York City for three decades. Sometimes, they would reminisce about the apartment on 145th Street and Lenox Avenue. Harlem wasn't like it is now, shopping and theatre. It had a different charm, I think. There were times when I could hear how they missed being there. So, two years ago, I thought it would be nice to take some pictures of the places they still love and remember, put some prose around them to tell a kind of people and places love story. It turned out to be a coffee table storybook. The project was huge and has taken most of my time here, but I learned a lot about the city. I've only got a few more edits to do before I get it off to the publisher."

We talked for hours and nibbled away at the dinner until she fell asleep curled into me on the sofa. I didn't have the heart to wake her.

§§§

After the other day with the females outside the store, I had to talk to someone. I liked Trinity Church, especially Reverend George who was nicer than the others were. He had always listened to me before.

Even though things had been going to shit, it seemed they were looking up when I walked in the church and saw the jasmine-smelling chick from the store sitting in the rear pew.

"Jasmine!" I said it like it was her name, like I knew her. She looked up, but waved me away...or tried to. *What the fuck is the waving about? Oh, she can smile all pretty for some chick, but she can't give me the time of day?*

"Lady, I know when I've seen a star."

This got her attention. *Worked every time.* All women want guys to tell them they're beautiful, even when they're butt ugly. This wasn't my first time.

"After all, beauty is in the eyes of, right?"

I figured I'd quote that guy I read. I don't remember his name, but it made her look up so now I could see her eyes. They were brown, kind of light and a pretty almond shape. The gun came away clean and her eyes went big for just a sec. I was happy it didn't snag on my jacket like the other times this week. Practicing the pull had felt clumsy until this moment. The fear in her eyes was dragging my day down again. So I pulled the trigger. It was easy. It felt smooth, like that car I used to drive—no rattle, just hum. Her face was gone in the next moment.

§§§

I can't remember if the feeling about her was immediate or not. We'd only been together a few weeks, but it had felt good. The conversation, the sex, the quiet moments all felt exactly as they should. It really was only about two months, but I missed her when she was gone, missed the smiles over dinner, the way she would stick just her toes out from under the blanket and tell me how cold the room was. I knew someone else might not find these things so cute, but I didn't care. I was going to ask her to stay with me tomorrow when we went to see the tree at Rockefeller Center.

When the phone rang, I couldn't even remember where it was. By the time I found it, I was completely bothered. *Who even had this number?*

"Hello?"

"Is this Ms. Charters?" The caller's voice had a craggy sound to it like he smoked too much or was losing the battle on a really bad sore throat.

"Yes. Who is this?"

"Detective Spinner, ma'am. Do you know a Chaun King?"

"What's happened?"

"Ms. King has you listed as next of kin."

§§§

Walking into the sanctuary, Iam realized there was a funny smell in the air. George and Louis had left by the side door and closed it firmly behind them. The candles weren't lit as of yet. *What a time for this to happen.* So many things were going wrong here at Trinity, the community didn't need any more problems and certainly, the ministry didn't. Between the thefts out of the lock box to the tune of five thousand dollars and the poor performance of the last fundraiser, the scaffolding surrounding the church might never come down. Iam was determined just to open the doors to let in some air when he saw a pair of legs sticking out of the pew closest to the rear door.

The smell grew significantly worse as he neared the body. Reaching for his cell phone, he realized the main doors were open, just a bit. Earlier in the day, he'd been sitting in the pew across from where the body now laid, admiring the majesty of the ceiling.

"Oh dear!" Iam's exclamation bore little resemblance to the immense feeling he had when he realized he was looking at Chaun King's body. She'd been responsible for the last successful fundraiser only two years ago and raised almost fifty thousand dollars. He could see the ear cuff on her left ear, the same one she wore in the picture with Reverends George and Louis. Since the last time he saw her, her locks had grown down past her shoulders.

"There's been a murder." He gave 911 the details and flipped his phone closed without giving his name. For a moment, he considered calling George and Louis. *They should know, should be here. But what could they do?* No, he would call them after the police left.

§§§

"Officer." The pudgy man sitting in the pew called to the arriving police.

"Sir, where is Reverend George?"

"Not here, I'm afraid."

"Reverends Charles or Louis?"

"Also not here."

"What is your name, sir?"

"Iam G."

Even though their notebooks were open, their pens in hand, they both stopped and gave the pudgy man a questioning look.

"Spell that, please?" Neither cracked a smile. They'd heard so many things over the years. Homicide brings out the crazies and the church is no protection against that.

"I-A-M-G" saying it slowly as he watched the officers write it down.

"Do you know where Reverends George or Louis are, Mr. G?"

"Please call me Iam. I'm sorry I didn't catch your names."

"Reese and Stuyvesant."

"I don't know where they are. They needed the night off and I was here." He answered with a shrug of his shoulders.

"Mr. G, can you tell us what happened?"

"Well, I don't really know. I was about to open the doors for the late afternoon service. I walked out from the office when I realized it was only fifteen minutes until they were scheduled to begin and as I walked to the doors I noticed a funny smell."

"Take your time, sir." Iam looked nervous.

"I noticed a smell and it became quite strong near the doors. I was going to call Reverend George when I saw Ms. King."

"Did you hear the shot?"

"No, I didn't. I don't know how I didn't, but..." Iam's voice trailed off as his eyes refocused on Chaun's legs.

"Were the doors locked?"

"I thought so, but when I called 911, I saw the main door was open a crack. I know George and Louis were arguing about locking them or not. George felt they shouldn't be locked. Said something about the church isn't a store only open for business at certain hours, but a place to minister to the needs of the community. Of course, that's not verbatim I only overheard the argument as I was walking in."

"Argument?"

"Yes, Reverends George and Louis were arguing when I arrived."

"They left you in charge, but didn't say where they were going?"

"They didn't have to. They are reachable by phone. Perhaps I should call them."

§§§

Weeks Later...

"Hello." Tracy hadn't meant to answer the phone, at least not consciously. It was Joe. She knew that if she didn't answer, he would keep calling.

"Tracy. It's me, Joe."

"Yeah, what's up?"

"I'm in the neighborhood—"

"Joe, I'm not in the mood—"

"I've got something to show you, so I hope you're dressed. This is important." Now, someone was knocking on her door. When she opened it, there stood Joe. Suddenly, she was angry. She hadn't felt that yet today. *What a slippery slope these emotions are.*

Joe walked into the apartment looking like he had just drank the bottle from the bottom up. Of course, this was *still* pretty good for him. Usually he was much closer to wasted.

"Joe, I'm serious. This is not the fucking time."

Friend or not, one of Joe's drunken visits was not on her list for today. She'd had to call Chaun's parents. She hadn't even met them and had to tell them some New York nutcase killed their daughter.

"Got any bourbon?"

"Why did that sound like a question?"

"Just being polite."

"Polite? Yeah, right."

He put the dirty paper bag on the counter and poured himself some, throwing it back faster than he'd poured the two-finger spread. He was all kinds of *fucked up*.

"What in this bag on the counter?" Tracy picked it up. "It weighs a ton."

The oil stains were dark and foreboding, if that's even possible.

She moved it from the counter because the oil stains looked like they might seep through. Joe, of course, was in the bathroom. She was beginning to think something else, besides drinking too much, was wrong with him.

"Joe?" Looking into the bag, Tracy learned early you'll buy your own bullshit pretty easily, but lately she'd been buying her neighbor's delusional shit, too. The gun made her eyes water or maybe it was the smell of the cleaning oil. She dropped it on the sofa.

Because Joe approached everything straight on like he was playing chicken with life, she was sure, he thought the gun would solve the problem. How he lived like that, she never understood. She dealt in the grey areas of life more often than not. Their differences worked as friends, most of the time, though not in this moment.

"Joe, look, I know you mean well, but really? Take it. I don't want it here."

She knew she couldn't possibly keep it. A gun fucked up her life by killing Chaun.

"Pour me some of that bourbon, will you? I need to sit down." He was the first person she called after talking with the detective because he listened. He listened even when her words filled her with blinding pain. Now he poured two more fingers while she told him the detective had called back to say some guy confessed.

"You know what I did yesterday?"

I waited, really looking for him to say something, anything before the bourbon warmed up my throat and melted my heart. But Joe didn't say a word.

"I started looking for a word stronger than hate because I wanted to write about it. A word, Joe." Tracy was filling with sarcasm as her anger turned inward. "Who looks for a word when someone they love is killed. What was I going to do with a word, lambast him in the press? No one gives a rat's ass about a man with a gun? They ran four, Joe, four short paragraphs in the paper. They didn't even bother with a follow-up. She didn't mean much to anyone but me. How do I live with that?" The tears ran down her face as Joe poured another shot.

"I tried to go to Trinity this morning. It seemed like a really good idea, you know, to talk with Reverend Louis. Maybe he could help me understand why this happened. I got as far as reaching for the doors, but I couldn't go in. Not yet."

"It's too soon." Joe said it like he knew my pain.

"They painted them white you know—the doors. Part of the rebuilding fund Chaun raised money for, I think."

Joe listened and drank with me. He was good like that. We'd be fucked up first thing in the morning, but really, who cares?

"Did I ever tell you, she used to do this thing on weekdays when we're both working on our projects? She'd send me a text to go the door and when I got there, I'd find she dropped off some lunch for me with a note saying she'd be back later. Sweet...that's what that was. How does so much happen in just a few weeks?"

"Two months," he said. "You were together two months."

"Joe—" He'd been counting, even when I wasn't.

"What were you doing when I called?"

"Nothing. Absofuckinglutely nothing. I was trying not to answer the phone. I don't want to remember the last two months. Maybe you could remember for me."

"You're kind of amazing that way, crazy but amazing because you listen to me. I'm going over to Trinity tomorrow. Just as soon as I wake up.

I must have passed out after that. I woke up to find I salt traces from my tears on my cheeks and the sofa pillows. I hadn't even made it to my bed. I could hear Joe messing with the pots in the kitchen.

"I am also going to see a therapist." I said it like I hadn't even passed out.

"You sure about that? You never seemed like the therapist type to me."

"Yeah, I'm sure. I can't sleep. The dreams are getting worse. The other night I dreamt the detective's call came in after I'd gone to bed for the evening, only the ringer was this shrill whistle like a teakettle. Then my dream had me at my desk talking with Chaun on the phone and when the phone rang in my hand, it was the detective telling me I was her next of kin. I'm afraid to sleep. I know it's going to take a while. I don't know what else to do. If I speak with Reverends George or Louis, maybe I wouldn't go to bed every night squeezing my eyes shut even while I'm afraid to keep them closed. I feel like there are bits and pieces being ripped directly from my heart. What the fuck?"

"I'll leave the bag under the sink, just in case..."

"Joe?"

He was closing the door behind him.

§§§

I wasn't going to make it walking over there, but I could call. Hangover or not, I needed answers.

"Good Morning, Sir. I wonder if you could direct me to Reverend George or Louis."

"Unfortunately, they are not here this morning. Perhaps I could be of service to you?"

"My name is Tracy Charters and—"

"My condolences, Ms. Charters."

"Thank you. I had hoped to speak with either of them. I understand the man who shot Chaun confessed."

"The detective called you then."

"Yes, were you there?" Tracy was hopeful. She needed answers and expected Reverend Louis could be the one to give them to her, but she'd talk with this man if it would help.

"The young man came in to see Reverend Louis. I asked Louis to come out to the sanctuary to meet his visitor. It was actually very timely on the part of the young man as Reverend Louis wasn't expected to be here. Both he and George had left to be with their families for a few days, but he stopped in because he forgot something."

"So it was coincidence?"

"Well, I guess so. I would say providence actually. Louis is called to minister. He would expect it to be no other way.

"Yes, well...providence then."

"You're not an active church member as Chaun was. It's all right, Ms. Charters. We are here for all who need us. I'm sorry, but as I stated earlier, Reverend Louis isn't here. Can I be of assistance?"

"I wanted to know what happened. They said her body was found there."

"Well, yes. I found her."

Hearing that, her tears spilled over and Tracy found herself crying soft, gasping sobs.

"I can try to answer your questions if you think you're up to it."

"Honestly I don't, but I have to know."

Iam repeated what he told the police detectives. He only left out how he'd recognized Chaun. He had no wish to for Tracy to suffer any more from the realization of the extensive damage the shot had done. He would spare her at least that much.

"Were you also there when he confessed?"

"I stepped away after Louis entered the sanctuary. I thought to give them some privacy. One never knows if the moment is a simple question or something much deeper.

I went only far enough to be out of earshot. When Louis took the young man's hands in his, I knew. "

"He confessed? Just like that?"

"Ms. Charters, I don't know that it was just like that. It didn't take long though. Perhaps the young man had set his intentions prior to entering the church. After all, he asked for Louis specifically."

"I'm sorry, Mr. G. Is it Reverend?"

"Please Iam would be fine. I'm not one for standing on ceremony."

"Iam, have you any idea what happens now that the police have him in custody?"

"I'm sorry, I don't. I minister to those in need and that is contrary to the court system. Their procedures are foreign to me."

"Thank you, Iam. Please tell Reverend Louis I'll stop in again soon."

§§§

"Afternoon, Detectives."

"Afternoon, Mr. G." Iam felt no need to correct the way they addressed him this time. He knew they wouldn't respond.

"We understand Ms. Charters was here to speak with you about Chaun King. What did she want?"

"And you know this how?" The detectives ignored his question.

"What did she want?"

"She had questions, but mostly I think she wanted to talk to someone, to try to understand what happened. From the circles under her eyes, I suspect she hasn't been sleeping very well. While she was here, she told me a story about Ms. King. She said, on Sundays she would sit in that very pew, eating the extra bagel from the three she bought for them for breakfast. She always ate the plain one in church so as not to disturb everyone with the smell of food. She was a very considerate young woman.

"This church has suffered a great loss, Detectives. Ms. King's activities with the church were a significant contribution to getting that awful scaffolding down and returning the majesty of the church to its rightful owners, the Portsborough Community.

"Anyway, I laughed a little as Ms. Charters told me the story. It seemed like she used to attend church as well, but hasn't found her way back to it just yet. We could use more members like Ms. King."

The detectives seemed a little exasperated. "You said she had questions?"

"Yes, she did."

"What were they?"

"Well really, just one. An eye for an eye or thou shalt not kill?"

§§§

Nervous wasn't a sufficient description for the energy Tracy felt walking into the courthouse. The arraignment for Chaun's killer was today and she promised herself that she would be there to see it.

The courthouse hallways were small with only a few benches between the heavy wooden doors. Not at all, like the TV version that showed plenty of space from wall to wall or person to person. This arraignment was part of a shorter process for her murderer. He had confessed. No trial for those who proclaim their guilt. Still her stomach fluttered as they all stood when the judge entered.

"If it may please the court?" His attorney started to speak and the butterflies in her stomach made swoops and dives. Tracy knew something wasn't right. The prosecutor looked confused and the judge had a look of wide-eyed curiosity. Something was terribly wrong and Tracy could feel it.

"We're requesting a dismissal of all charges, Your Honor."

"A dismissal?" The prosecutor's look went from confusion to shock.

The judge asked his clerk if this was the right case. Was this in fact, Cisco Allston before him? The clerk nodded.

"Approach."

A few minutes passed. The judge looked quite annoyed and the prosecutor vigorously shook his head from side to side while they conversed with the defense attorney.

"Step back, both of you."

"Mr. Allston, I don't know how this error occurred and if I had my way, you would be sent away for a very long time. However, it seems the circumstances of this case prevent that. You are free to go. Case dismissed." The bang of the gavel bounced around the room as if the base was connected to surround-sound speakers. He walked past me...free. *Unfuckingbelievable.*

Dazed, I called Joe.

"What's up?"

"He's free."

"What?" She could hear the outrage in his voice. "Seriously?"

"Yes, freer than the birds in the fucking sky. He walked out of the courtroom not five minutes ago. The judge was annoyed. Said circumstances prevented him from moving further with the case. The prosecutor grumbled his understanding and then it was done. I can't believe it!"

"It's public record, right? So you need to find out what happened."

"Yeah, I know, but can you believe they dismissed the case? He confesses to killing Chaun and is in jail for what, seventy two hours tops?"

"Tracy! Tracy! You are not listening to me. Find out what happened."

"Right, I hear you. I need a drink."

"Info, then drink." He hung up. *I don't know why I called him, like there was something he could do.* Talking to him frustrated me every time.

Apparently, an admission of guilt sometimes isn't always admissible. At the time of his arrest, the gun was not on his person. There were no witnesses to the shooting. The minister at the church didn't see him there except when he came in to speak to Reverend Louis. Officers questioned passersby, neighboring businesses and no one remembered seeing Cisco Allston at the scene or near it. And what were the grounds for dismissing his case? His confession! His attorney's argument indicated his right to privacy had been violated since he confessed to Reverend Louis and not to a police officer.

According to the papers filed, Cisco entered Trinity Episcopal and asked for Reverend Louis. During the conversation with Reverend Louis, Cisco Allston mentioned he was sorry he shot the woman he called Jasmine. Reverend Louis talked to him for a little while and then Mr. Allston called the police.

At no time did Mr. Allston tell the police that he shot Ms. King, only that he'd said so to Reverend Louis.

§§§

Tracy needed to understand how could this happen and headed back to the church. She found Iam sitting in the last pew, almost as if he was waiting for her.

"Iam, do you remember speaking with me?"

"Yes, of course, Ms. Charters. How are you feeling?"

"About the same, Iam. The case against Cisco Allston was dismissed yesterday."

"I hadn't heard. I'm sorry, Ms. Charters. I know you had hoped things would be taken care of in court."

"Yes, yes I had."

"But how can I help you now?"

"What did the guy, Cisco, say when he was here? Did he say why?"

"Ms. Charters, I saw him talking with Reverend Louis as I mentioned before. Had I overheard what was said I could not reveal the details. This job is often a difficult one as we minister to all who seek it, including those who take the lives of others."

"I don't understand why they let him go today."

"The seal, perhaps."

"The seal?"

"Yes, the seal of confession. When this Cisco Allston confessed to Reverend Louis, he must have done so as an act of contrition."

"And this means he walks free?"

"I cannot say that it means that, no. I am not an attorney, but it does mean Reverend Louis cannot testify against him, cannot serve as a witness to what was said. He is bound not to reveal the content of the conversation."

"But you heard him as well."

"No, but it would not matter. I am also bound"

"I thought that if a person confesses to crimes like murder there were exceptions."

"There are no exceptions to the seal."

§§§

The Clinton Avenue Bar is about midway between Tracy's apartment and Trinity Episcopal Church. She and Joe used say the block was an excellent combination of spirits and beers. Spirit number three was on its way to Joe's table when Tracy walked in.

"What did you find?"

"Reverend Louis is apparently a good listener, too good. He was the only one listening when Cisco Allston, that's the murderer's name, walked in feeling like he wanted to talk to someone. This other minister, Iam, I know, crazy name, was there, but stepped away to give them privacy. Anyway, I ran a background check and found some basic info; old addresses and phone numbers.

"So then Mr. G, uh, Reverend G tells me about this seal of confession. I tell him I thought confessions were within the confessional box, but apparently, the sanctity of the church and the seeming admission of contrition regarding the sin is enough. I don't know if it's always enough, but in this case, it was. He told me neither he nor Reverend Louis would be able to confirm or deny the confession. Basically, it was a whopper of a technicality that this guy must have known about or else he wouldn't have confessed. I don't know what he got out of this, but I'm going to find out."

"Really, Iam?" Joe heard every word, but was stuck on the pudgy guy's name.

"Round 4?" We ordered more drinks. The discussion ahead of us was going to be rough.

§§§

There's a way you can move about the day without recognizing what it is you're doing or where you are. I spent those days after the court appearance trying to figure out what to do next. I found I had too much time on my hands, so I tried to do laundry to tidy things up until I found her shirt still smelling lightly of sweat and the vanilla scent she used to oil her locks.

Walking outside proved fruitless, the sun's rays had no effect on my mood. Clinton Avenue Bar was open, but one look at my reflection and I turned back toward the apartment. I'd had enough. The drink left me with a headache that hurt almost as much as the memory of Chaun.

Standing on the platform at Clinton-Lafayette Avenues waiting for the C train, I looked up to see Cisco walking through the turnstile. I hadn't seen him since he was set free. I was surprised to see him going about his life without a care in the world. What care would he have? He was a free man.

I stepped onto the train two doors down from him and almost lost sight of him when he moved into the center of the car. He's a short man. I guess I hadn't realized it until then. But now from here, I could tell he probably wasn't more than 5'6". He was actually a small man. The shoulders that seemed so wide from my seat in the galley of the courtroom were only a tad bit wider than my own. He jostled passengers without a care as he moved to the exit at West 4th Street.

I had no idea what I was really doing, following behind him as he walked east on West 4th Street. He waved at the people in the garage on the left and mentioned he'd be right back before he walked over to the cleaners.

Even as I reached for the phone to call Joe, I knew I was making some sort of a decision. *Had this been what he was doing when he shot Chaun? Watching her?*

"Joe. Hey, I'm going to need your help."

"Whatever you need."

"I was heading into the city and Cisco walked into the subway station, so I followed him."

"Crazy, but fortunate."

"Yeah, it was, wasn't it? I think I hoped his life would be less than normal. You know, like he wandered the streets, didn't have a home because he was crazy, violent, something. Instead, he rides the subway, chats with his co-workers and has his clothes dry-cleaned. He's just like us."

"No, not just like us. He's an uncertified nut case."

"I watched him, Joe. Watched him as he read his book on the train, basically riding the subway without a care in the world. Who does that when just three weeks ago they walked up to a woman in a church and shot her in the face?"

"Where's he work?"

"A garage near MacDougal and West 4th Street."

"Like a parking garage?"

"Yeah."

"What time did he get there?"

"Just before 8 a.m."

"I'm guessing he didn't see you."

"If he did, he didn't care because he waved at his co-workers and chatted up the folks at the cleaners like it was just another day."

"Let's see what happens tomorrow morning."

I have a singular purpose most times—get to the point, quickly and cleanly. My friends say when we were kids and all the other kids would be arguing over who was going to go first, even arguing over who was going to flip the coin to see who was going to go first. I would just flip the coin and piss everybody off, but at last, the game would start. Seemed like a stupid argument. Who cares who goes first?

§§§

Tracy needed my help with this. I could hear that and so could she. Why else would she call me, talk with me about following this guy? I hate him too because he fucked with Tracy's happiness. Just three months ago, Tracy was one happy-ass female. She and Chaun were attached at the hip right away and not in a bad way. Smiling and joking, giving each other a reason to get up in the morning.

She didn't have to tell me their sexual chemistry was off the charts because every time I saw them, I could feel it. They would look for each other in a room ever so often and smile. To me, it always looked like they were sharing a memory of a moment. It felt as if they were alone, unaware there were others in the room.

That and we'd been friends for a long time. So I was there for her, whatever.

§§§

"Z, what's up? Thanks for the tools, man. They worked really well. Good lookin' out."

"Cool."

"You around for a bit? Thinking about dropping by your place."

"Yeah, man. Drop by whenever. I'm here all day." Z hung up the phone, half expecting Cisco to knock on the door right away. He always seemed to be just outside when he'd called in the past.

Cisco arrived at Z's with a six-pack and popped the top off one before the lid closed on the trashcan. His day had seemed longer than usual. He'd found himself distracted with the memory of shooting the lesbian chick in the church. The ease of it had felt kinda good to him, like it was supposed to be. Maybe he'd finally figured out what he was supposed to do.

"Yo, Z, about that chick I told you about a while back. You know the lesbian one talking like a dude to her girl?"

"What about her?"

"I saw her again. She was in Trinity Church. At first, I thought she was there to ask for forgiveness or something. She was sitting in the back waiting to talk to the Reverend, so I went over to her first thing. Figured it was a good time, you know?"

"Uh-huh."

"Anyway, you listening, man?"

"Yeah, I'm listening. Fucking remote isn't working right." Z was messing with the batteries in the remote. "So you went over and...?"

"She wouldn't talk to me, wouldn't even give me a chance. I don't understand it."

"Cis, hand me a beer."

Z flipped the remote over to see if rolling the batteries around worked when Cisco put the beer down.

"So?" The question hung in the air until Z looked up at Cisco and saw him point to his head with his index finger and flex his thumb.

"Shit, man, you didn't." It wasn't really that Z didn't believe Cisco could do it. On the contrary, he knew Cisco was a crazy motherfucker, but in a church? He shot her in a church! Even though he'd seen the article a few weeks before, but he didn't think for a second it could have been him.

"Fuckin' lesbian acted like I wasn't good enough. Tried to wave me off like I was interrupting her moment when all she was doing was sitting in the back of the church eating a bagel."

Z was shaking his head.

"I just brought that gun up here. It was clean. That's the loss of a good piece." Z voice was somewhat sad because it takes a lot of work to get a clean gun.

"It's not lost. I liked it too much to get rid of it."

Even as he flicked through the channels, Z could tell something was off. Cisco was not acting like himself. Z settled on a sports channel, put the remote down and watched Cisco instead of the game. *Something definitely wasn't right.*

"Hey Cis, you know the manager says there's a new guy yesterday. I'd like it if you showed him round the first couple of days. His name's Joe Drexer. Drives everything, or so he says."

"Okay, when does he start?"

"He'll be here at 9:00 a.m. sharp."

"I didn't know we needed a new guy? The place is kinda slow now."

Cisco didn't really care, but the manager seemed to like it when he made conversation so that's what he did.

"Friend of the owners called, said they were sending somebody down to learn the ropes. Probably some rich guy's son looking to jerk off for the school break."

"Yeah, probably."

$$\$\$\$$$

Right before nine, Joe walked into the garage. He hadn't had a drink since yesterday afternoon and it showed. He looked tired. "Can't drive cars drunk," she'd said. "If you're going to do this, you're going to have to hold off on the liquor. When I asked how she swung the job for me so fast, she told me she had checked out the owner info and just said I was a friend of the owner's son. Figured it was good for a week before payroll.

"Hey! You know where the manager is?"

"How do you know I'm not the manager?" Cisco asked, being a bit peeved because this guy didn't think it was him.

"Didn't think. Sorry, you the manager?"

"Nah, he's in the back. Said you were starting this morning and that I should show you around."

"Cool. Someplace I can drop this bag? Lots of books."

Cisco smiled and pointed to the back.

"In the manager's office."

"Be right back."

"Hey! Nothing much going on here. Boss sits around more than he works. A car comes in occasionally and whoever is near the front parks it. We start the same time every day and leave the same time. Schedule never changes.

Joe called Tracy to tell her to "Drive that piece a shit car into the garage tomorrow morning at 9:15 and I'll park it for you. That's Cisco's coffee break."

§§§

"Cisco Barnes, 28, of Portsborough, N.Y., was found shot to death Tuesday in the West Street parking garage in New York City where he had worked as a parking attendant for the past year.

The shooting occurred around 9:30 a.m. Garage Manager Patrick Hauser said he was in his office reconciling the books at the time. 'I heard a bang, but that's not unusual here. Cars make all kinds of noises, so I didn't bother checking.'

Hauser said Barnes was friendly and quiet. 'I can't imagine he had any enemies.' The New York City Police said no witnesses have come forward and no weapon has been found. Anyone with information is asked to contact the police department."

IN THIS LIFE
JEAN HOLLOWAY

CHAPTER ONE

Cameo Griffith hurried through the white double doors into Trinity Episcopal Church and looked up past the massive wood beams to the highest point of the vaulted ceiling. Though the church was small in diameter, the pristine ivory walls and highly polished pews gave it a grand, pious air. After the long walk on the snowy city street, she stood for a moment and leaned against the door. She pulled her vintage Jaeger Black leather maxi coat tighter. Although it was noticeably warmer inside than out on this frigid morning. On the Saturday before Christmas Eve, the church seemed deserted. Everyone must be doing last minute shopping or spending time with family.

She thought that once inside it would give her some feeling of relief, however that didn't happen. The crisp light of the winter morning shone through the stained glass windows and lit up the sanctuary with hues resembling a Thomas Kinkade classic, but its beauty went unnoticed. Cameo genuflected, made the sign of the cross and ducked behind the black curtain of the confessional without looking for a priest. She wanted to take this directly to God with no middleman interference. Besides, in this particular situation, she couldn't really trust a priest now, could she?

"Forgive me, Father, for I have sinned." But had she, really? After all, it had not happened yet. "This is my first confession. I accuse myself of the following sins..." She found it difficult to go any further, to say the word "murder." It seemed impossible that she was going to bear the responsibility of a man's death. But didn't Exodus 21:24 say, "Eye for eye, tooth for tooth, hand for hand, foot for foot?" A life for a life surely followed. Before she continued, Cameo thought back on how it all began...

§§§

It started out as such an adventure. Her dad had gotten a new job as Operations Manager on the dock of the East Bank and to celebrate she and her mom were going to spend the day window shopping and perhaps take in a movie. They would meet up for supper when Dad's shift ended and take the ferry home together.

She stood on deck of the ferry, looking at the peaceful river when suddenly it swept over the bow and pummeled the ship's sides, rocking it so steeply that gallons of water poured in. She held on to her father's hand as her parents rushed to the deck. People were running and screaming, panicked at the sudden certainty of a watery death. In all the commotion, her hand slipped and she suddenly became separated from her family. Cameo added her scream to the screams of the crowd and the already deafening sounds of the sinking ship. Everyone was pushing and several punches were thrown as the crew fought to get into the lifeboats. Apparently the "women and children first" rule did not apply here.

The frigid water rose over her feet and she looked down, surprised to see how pale they looked in the moonlit night. She saw that the backs of her hands were white, too. She seemed so small as she slipped in and out of the mob of people trying to make her way to the railing and reach the lifeboats. She was almost there when the strange man grabbed her by the shoulders and pulled her away.

"Come here, girl," he commanded and began dragging her towards the other side of the deck where the automobiles were parked.

"No! Let go of me! I have to find my parents," Cameo screamed, struggling to break free from his grasp.

Everyone was so concerned with their own dilemma that no one paid the two of them any attention. He took advantage of the situation, picked her up and carried her to a 1970 Ford Country Squire station wagon. He held her by the neck with his forearm while unlocking the three-way magic door and then threw her into the cargo area behind the back seat. The stranger ripped off her dress and forced his knee between her legs. He had just begun to penetrate her when a gush of water swept the car off the deck and into the water, but he continued as if nothing would prevent him from completing his mission. The man continued to force himself on her and as the water quickly seeped in and began to flood the car, he held her down, hurting her, raping her.

She could smell dust with a slight hint of mothballs on his clothes. The water rushed in the open windows and covered her body. Floating above her attacker was darkness in the form of a shadow. It resembled the outline of a very large man. Afraid, she looked down from the apparition and saw her attacker's features, contorted with lust. He now resembled the monster he had become. She looked up into his face one last time and then the rising water forced her to close her eyes.

A glimpse of color popped into her peripheral vision and caught her attention. A red and white striped life preserver with the name of MV George Prince stamped on it floated by the car window and she watched it as it appeared to rise. In actuality, it was the distance that grew between them as the car sank further into the river. As he began to climax, he grabbed her throat, his hands and the incoming water choking her, silencing her screams...

Suddenly Cameo woke up sweating, coughing and fighting the covers, her hands cold and clammy. Without thinking, she rubbed them together, warming them. It was always the same damn nightmare. It felt very different from her normal dreams. These had overly bright colors that reminded her of high definition TV and her perspective felt as if she were actually there, watching instead of dreaming. Cameo wondered what it all meant.

She got out of her canopy bed and stumbled into the bathroom. Looking in the mirror at her oval face with its dark chocolate color, her reflection reassured her that she had not turned Caucasian overnight. Funny, the change of race didn't faze her in the nightmare. It somehow felt right. Her worry hadn't been the color of her skin, but the horror of the man attacking her. This time, after she shook the dread her nightmare created, she clearly remembered the ship's name. Since it was Saturday, she decided to do a little investigating to see if a ship by that name had ever actually existed.

Cameo showered and dressed. After making a breakfast sandwich of ham, egg and cheese on toast and coffee, she drove to the library. Logging on to one of their computers, she googled the ship's name and the amount of information that came tumbling out completely surprised her. MV George Prince had been a ferry in Louisiana. Now Cameo wondered if the girl in her dream was Caucasian, Cajun or Creole. There had to be a way to find out.

Was it a coincidence that the ferry accident occurred on Wednesday, October twentieth, nineteen seventy-six at six fifteen a.m. while traveling from the West to the East Bank of the Mississippi River? It had been hit by a Norwegian tanker and sunk, just as it had in her dream. If that was real, what else was true? Why was there no mention of a little girl? In all the commotion, had someone gotten away with rape and murder that night? The fact that her birth certificate stated that she had come into this world exactly one hour later made it all the more eerie.

She read through the passenger manifest, whispering their names aloud with the hope that one might spark some recognition. The deceased and the survivors were all listed, however none of their names rang a bell. Reaching a dead end, Cameo decided she needed to talk to her mother. Leaving the library, she jumped into her silver 1995 Dodge Avenger. Pulling her cell out of her purse, she called her Mom to let her know she would stop by and headed straight for her parents' home.

Her mother answered the door wearing a coral velour housecoat and her hair held back with a matching headband. Before she could say a word, Cameo rushed in, wrapped her arms around her, buried her face in the warmth of her mother's lavender-scented neck and burst into tears.

"What is it, Honey?"

She led Cameo to the burgundy corduroy couch and continued to hold her until the tears subsided and waited while her daughter composed herself enough to start asking questions.

"Momma, tell me about the morning I was born."

"What? What do you want to know?"

"Was there anything strange about it?"

"Strange, like how, baby?"

"I don't know? I mean, were there any problems?"

"No, in fact, you were in such a rush to be born; you came out fighting right after my water broke. Unlike most babies, you were screaming before the doctor had a chance to smack your cute little tush. Your face was so flushed, at first he worried that your umbilical cord might be choking you, but you were just fine."

"The doctor thought I was choking?" Could that be another coincidence?

"It wasn't serious. Why? What brought all this on? Why were you crying?"

"I don't want you to think I'm crazy."

"Too late."

Her mother's chuckle brought a slight smile to Cameo's tear-stained face. She slowly began to tell her about the strange nightmare and finished her story with what she had discovered online at the library.

"So what are you saying? You think you were that little girl? How's that possible? Honey, we've never even been to Louisiana."

"I know, but how would I know the name of the ship?"

"Okay, I'll admit, it is a little strange. Maybe you saw something on TV like, I don't know, folks in Louisiana making preparations for some kind of twenty-fifth-year anniversary memorial or something?"

"Yeah, maybe that was it," Cameo answered, lying to them both.

CHAPTER TWO

Her emotional conversation with her mother had not answered any of her questions. In fact, it only created more. On the drive back home, she made one more call. He answered on the first ring.

"Hey, baby, what's up?"

"Josh, I need to talk to you. Can I come over?"

"Sure, you sound a little down. Are you okay?"

"Yeah, well, as good as can be expected, I guess. I'll explain it all when I get there."

"Maybe I can do something to cheer you up?"

"Maybe, you can. I'll be there in a half hour."

He opened the door before she could ring the bell and just the sight of his six-foot, well-muscled frame and handsome milk chocolate face eased her confusion a little. He must have seen her distraught look because he wrapped his arm around her and ushered her past the sunlight foyer into his living room. They sat together on his denim loveseat and he took her hand.

"Okay, Cam, tell me what's going on?"

She told him the whole story from the beginning, how the nightmares began shortly before her twenty-first birthday, up to her earlier visit with her mother. Cameo didn't know what reaction she expected. It could be anything from Josh thinking it could be some kind of joke or believing she might be crazy; but when she finished, he pulled her so close she could smell the faint scent of Grabbazi cologne and then he whispered in her ear.

"So, when are we leaving for Louisiana?"

At that very moment, she loved him more than she thought possible.

§§§

Joshua listened to her amazing story and found himself at a loss for words. Did she actually believe she had been a murder victim in a prior life? Sure, he knew more people in the world believed in reincarnation than in Christianity, but that didn't hold true for most African Americans. As he held her, he felt her trembling subside. She looked up into his face and her full lips drew him in. Their passionate kiss quickly got out of control and the next thing he knew, they were undressing each other, his hands unbuttoning her blouse, her hands reaching for his zipper, their zeal overwhelming their vow to stay celibate until marriage. It took every ounce of willpower he had to pull himself away from her.

"What are we doing? What happened to doing it old school and waiting?"

"Josh, I need you. Help make me feel alive. I'm afraid."

Her words stirred within him such feelings of protectiveness that he was forced to reconsider his lust. She was in a vulnerable state and didn't need anything else adding to her stress. If they made love now, he feared she would soon regret it. With that thought, although his body protested, his mind helped him gently push her away.

"Josh? Why did you stop? What's wrong?" Her passion made the questions come out in short gasps.

"We shouldn't be doing this. What happened to our promise to wait? This isn't the way we wanted it to be."

Joshua Palmer was a self-made, common sense kind of guy. Although his high IQ got him an academic scholarship, he blew it after some rocky years of bad decisions made in his late teens to mid-twenties. Finally, the light bulb came on and he got himself together, but not before he was expelled from LaGuardia Community College and it cost him a free college education. He stopped the partying and drinking, even gave up weed and got his first job as construction help because he thought it might be fun playing with all the massive equipment. But he started as a day laborer and graduated to the go-to guy, first for coffee and architectural plans then setting up meetings with inspectors and hiring day laborers. In other words, he learned the administrative side of construction.

While dealing with the humdrum, he discovered his love of architecture. At twenty-seven, his new love spurred him to go back to college, working his way through the prestigious Pratt Institute. He did so well the first two years, Smith Concrete Construction footed half of his tuition bill for the last three and sponsored him through his post-graduate years. At thirty-four, he had just begun his senior year and was on his way to obtaining his Masters. Right now, he felt lucky in life and love. Everything was going his way. That's why Joshua couldn't believe what he was saying. She had definitely made him a changed man.

During his youth, he considered himself such a cocksmith that he lost track of all the women he had been to bed with. Luckily, to his knowledge, he hadn't fathered any children. Then something hit him right after his thirtieth birthday and he decided he wanted his life to amount to more than nights of meaningless lust. He noticed Cameo a couple of months later...

He spotted her one afternoon in Italia, a little Italian restaurant he frequented for lunch. Standing behind her in line, her thick, curvaceous body made the view from the back quite appealing. When she turned to reach for silverware, she bumped into him and her dark eyes and apologetic smile caught his attention.

"Excuse me," she said in a sweet, soft-spoken tone. Their eyes met and his stomach fluttered.

"Don't worry about it," was all he could think to say.

For weeks, he returned to the restaurant and tried to get up the courage to speak to her. Sometimes, she wouldn't be there and he would lose his appetite. Something about her made him a little shy and that alone piqued his interest. Usually, he came off as quite the ladies' man and always had a smooth line, but something about her, left him a little tongue-tied. He'd never had that reaction to a woman before.

One afternoon when the place was especially crowded, he saw her eating alone and grabbed his chance. He approached her.

"Well, hello again, pretty lady. My name's Josh…Joshua Palmer. Would you mind sharing your table? I've never seen Italia this packed."

§§§

Cameo looked up into his dark bronze face, quickly swallowed her lasagna and almost choked. With a wave of her hand, she indicated he should sit down. At a loss for words, her eyes quickly scanned his body and she noticed his muscled arms and his hair, done in well-groomed twists. Not bad!

"Hello Joshua, I'm Cameo Griffith. I know, huh? I guess my secret's out."

"Your secret?"

"Yeah, I can remember when no one knew about this place although I've noticed you've been coming here pretty regularly lately."

She'd spoken too quickly, without thinking. Now he knew she had seen him, too.

"I've been trying to work up the nerve to talk to you."

"You weren't afraid of me, were you?"

"Not afraid, I just didn't want to intrude on your lunch. How's the lasagna?"

"Fantastic as usual, what did you get?"

"Pork chop masala, their Tuesday special. It's great. Care for a bite?"

"Sure."

He swirled a little angel hair pasta and added a small portion of meat on his fork and fed it to her, watching her mouth open to receive his gift.

She tasted it, closing her eyes while she relished the taste. Her head nodded in agreement.

He waited until she finished chewing.

"I assume you work in the area?"

"Yeah, I'm a programmer at the Public Library, and you?"

"I'm working on my Masters at Platt."

"Very impressive."

"Well, I hope it will be when I graduate."

And so began the easiest conversation he had ever experienced. They met for lunch a couple of times before he got up the nerve to ask her out on a real date. The following Saturday at eight, he picked her up at her tiny studio apartment and did it properly, not just honking the car horn to let her know he was out front, but going to her front door and ringing the bell. She let him in and he saw that her taste revolved around earth tones, just like his.

They went to see "The Best Man" and then he splurged and took her to Napier's Bistro. He enjoyed the movie, the dinner and her company.

Less than a month into their relationship, she confided that she'd been celibate after a nasty breakup the previous year and concluded that revelation with the fact that she intended to stay that way until marriage. At first, he doubted her sincerity, but after a hot session that ended with her making him leave, he realized she took her vow seriously. Turned out she took everything seriously, so the fact that she talked to him about reincarnation meant she believed in it. And that's why he suggested their trip to Louisiana.

"We can make a vacation out of it, go to Mardi Gras."

"I've never been," he admitted aloud while thinking about how interesting it would be to see her in the partying atmosphere after several drinks. He hoped it would loosen her inhibitions and give him a chance to see a side of her she had never before revealed.

While she waited for their vacation, she found herself becoming obsessed with the mysteries of death. Whenever her mind wasn't occupied, random questions of the how, when and where she would take her final breath popped in. And what happens after death? Would she grow wings, get a harp and fly or go down that long tunnel toward the white light where family and friends awaited her arrival? She even secretly tried communicating with her late Grandma, but she wasn't as psychic as she would have liked to be.

Each night, she would try to revive her nightmare, hoping she would get additional clues to the man's identity, but she had no control over her dreams. All she could do was wait.

CHAPTER THREE

The smooth two and a half hour flight from JFK to New Orleans would have been enjoyable if it weren't for the butterflies flitting around in her sour stomach. Cameo feigned sleep for most of it and only "woke up" to ask the attendant for some ginger ale. It didn't help and while she sipped it, Teena Marie's "I've Been Here Before" began streaming from her headphones. The song only made her stomach flutters worse.

When they landed, they got into their waiting shuttle. After a half hour, the driver pulled up right on Orleans Street in front of the soft, olive green exterior of the Bourbon Orleans Hotel, an extremely elegant hotel infused with European flare. Even though it wasn't her style, the old world charm impressed her.

They checked in and were shown to their guestroom. Their queen-size room overlooked the vacant pool. When Joshua gave the bellman a tip at the door, she heard him ask Joshua if they had purchased the haunted New Orleans package.

"Haunted? You're saying this hotel is haunted?"

She could hear the disbelief in Joshua's voice. If he doesn't believe in ghosts, does he believe in reincarnation? Is he just humoring his crazy girlfriend?

"Well, sir, we've had reports of sightings, from children to nuns to gentleman callers. It's said they used to hold séances here."

"We bought the Mardi Gras package. All we're looking for is a good time."

That wasn't entirely true. But she didn't say a word.

With key in hand, they rode up the elevator. When Joshua opened the door to the room and Cameo strolled in, she felt like she had gone back in time.

After unpacking, they went down to the Bourbon Oh! Lounge and ordered a couple of VooDoo Mojo drinks, walked to Bubba Gump's where they shared steamed shellfish and a chocolate chip cookie sundae. After dinner, with a drink in hand, they joined the droves of people who had already started to party. Cameo and Joshua walked around the French Quarter, watched the brightly colored parades and listened to jazz and zydeco until they were both ready to turn in. She changed into her vintage shell pink, long satin-like polyester night gown and watched him get into the double bed near the door before she got into her bed down by the window.

As Cameo dozed off, she felt a light peck on her cheek.

"I love you too," she whispered.

"Huh?"

She opened her eyes to see Joshua lying under the covers in his own bed. The hairs on her arms rose.

"Did you just kiss me?"

"What are you talking about?"

"Well, someone did. I felt it."

"Maybe it was one of the so-called ghost guests?" He said jokingly and chuckled, but she did not join in.

"Can I get in bed with you?"

"I don't think that's a good idea. I mean, we're both buzzin'."

"We're also both adults. Besides, I trust you and I'm really a little scared."

Cameo hopped out of bed, crossed in front of the nightstand, sat on the side of Joshua's bed, tilted her head, raised her left eyebrow and gave him an imploring look.

"Okay, but you sure don't make things easy. Come on, get in."

He pulled back the covers and Cameo lifted her legs and got into his bed. Lying on her back with her right arm by her side and the left resting across her chest, it took her almost two hours to relax, but Josh's warmth and steady breathing, along with the alcohol, finally lulled her to sleep.

She had no idea how long she'd been asleep before she felt his hands on her, first on her knee, then slightly higher. Cameo took a deep breath and noticed the air had turned thick with humidity. She looked upward in a panic and saw the oddly familiar dark shadow of her dreams floating against the white ceiling. Terror rushed through her body and she became intensely aware of the sound of dripping water. The speed of the falling drops accelerated each time Joshua's hand inched higher and suddenly she realized she couldn't move. Cameo tried to turn her head and found that the paralysis covered her entire body.

The waning moon provided almost no light, but she caught a glistening of motion in the corner of her eye. Looking towards it, she realized she could still control their movement and that provided a modicum of relief until she realized drops of water were traveling across the ceiling, collecting in a pool over her face and then dropping into her eyes, blinding her, yet only her face was getting wet and the drops somehow seemed heavier than normal water.

The rest of her body felt hot and dry as his hand inched up her leg. Cameo lay immobilized. She tried to scream and tell him to stop, but all she could hear was a faint, rasping sound coming from her throat. He lifted her left arm as if to get it out of his way and turned over on her. They were face to face, his body blocking the dripping water and the shadow above him. Her vision cleared and when she looked into Joshua's eyes, they were glazed and unfocused. His irises appeared to be opaque and had gone from brown to a shiny black. In that instant, Cameo was certain that somehow it wasn't Joshua. He inhaled deeply and she could feel him sucking the breath from her soul. She tried to inhale, but he was pulling the air from deep inside her. She could feel it leaving her lungs and she began to suffocate. The room spun, adding to her nausea.

She felt his manhood push up against her pelvis and then pressure drove what little air she had left out of her as he began to penetrate. Miraculously, he suddenly snapped out of it and the dripping water stopped. The shadow abruptly vanished into the ceiling like a fur ball in a vacuum cleaner. Totally alert, Joshua's eyes and mouth opened wide with horror.

"Oh my God, Cam, I didn't mean, I'm sorry, I..."

Whatever was restraining her let go and she immediately took a deep breath, balled up her small fists and began beating Joshua on his head and shoulders. He had to grab both of her arms and pin them over her head to stop her. She stopped and felt the fight leave her body. Shaking her head "no," Cameo burst into tears and whispered, "I know it wasn't you."

"What the hell are you talking about, it wasn't me? I was on top of you, raping you! I don't know what happened. I can't explain it, I mean I didn't...I'm so sorry, Cam. I would never hurt you, I swear!"

"Josh, I looked into your eyes and they were empty, like your soul was gone. I know that whatever it was, it tried to suck the life out of me. But it wasn't you, Josh. You can let me go now, I'll be okay."

He did and they sat together on the side of his bed. Josh buried his head in his hands.

"We have to get out of here," Cameo flatly stated.

"You want to leave? Now?"

"I can't sleep here. We have to move to another hotel."

"Cam, please, I know this is bad, but finding another hotel with a vacancy at this late date is not going to be easy. Its Mardi Gras and you know that all the hotels are booked to capacity. It's gonna be impossible."

"I don't care, Joshua. Something or someone in this room made this happen. There's no way in hell I'll be able to stay here tonight.

Let's go down to the concierge's desk, ask for their help and see if they have any suggestions. We have to at least try, don't we?"

§§§

He watched her walk to the bathroom and close the door. What the hell just happened? Joshua agonized, remembering what he had tried to do. The guilt from waking up inside her weighed heavily on his soul. And when she returned to the bedroom, he could tell she had difficulty looking him in the eyes. It was almost as if she somehow felt responsible for his actions. Both of them dressed quickly and then rode together in the elevator to the lobby without saying another word.

With less than forty-eight hours before the official start of Mardi Gras, locating a vacant hotel room was impossible. All the decent hotels were booked to capacity.

Joshua grabbed her arm and pulled her aside.

"Look, we tried, babe, but there's nowhere we can go tonight. It's four a.m. We're just gonna have to tough it out and find something later."

"I am not going back to that room, Joshua. I would think you'd feel the same way." Cameo walked back to the concierge's desk. "Is someone here 24/7?"

"Yes, madam, especially during Mardi Gras."

"Can you get me a blanket?"

"Pardon?" The concierge looked the woman up and down, taking in her small stature and shapely body.

"I had a rather unsettling experience in our room and if I have to spend the night in this hotel, I'll do it camped out on one of your cozy chairs." Joshua got to her in time to hear the end of her sentence.

"You are NOT sleeping in the lobby. That's crazy."

"Oh, so my kind of crazy is fine when it excuses your behavior?"

"What the hell are you talking about?"

"Well, when my crazy ass suggested that you weren't responsible for trying to rape me, that was fine, but now that I..."

"Keep your voice down, Cam!"

"Don't tell me to keep it down. I'm not some kid. And the only reason I'll go back to that room is to pack. Now do I get that blanket or not?" She directed her question at the concierge. "I promise I'll stay out of sight, but please don't make me go back into that room tonight."

Looking from Cameo to Joshua, the concierge shrugged his shoulders and made the call to request the blanket.

CHAPTER FOUR

About three hours later, Cameo woke up to the low vroom of a vacuum cleaner. Sleeping in the chair had left her muscles aching and stiff. She stood up, stretched, folded the blanket and took it back to the concierge. Using her key card, she quietly re-entered their room, walked over to the sleeping Joshua and sat on the bed next to him.

"Mornin', Josh, time to get up.' She touched his cheek and he jumped up, shaking.

"Woman, you scared the shit out of me. What time did you come back to the room?"

"I just got here. Figured as long as we're here we might as well shower, get dressed, check out and go down by the Mississippi River bank. Take a look around."

"So you still want to go through with that?"

"Of course, you know that's why I'm here. I'm not gonna let anything stop me from trying to find that horrible man in my nightmare."

They packed up and brought their suitcases to the rental car. Cameo stayed in the passenger seat while Joshua settled the hotel bill. She couldn't resist the urge to turn around and glance back at the hotel. In a second floor window facing the street, she thought she caught a glimpse of a black silhouette. It appeared to duck out of sight as if to avoid being seen. The fact that the shadow's face had no features and she could see the interior of the room through it made her shiver, but she kept that to herself and said nothing when Joshua returned and got behind the wheel.

They made the half hour drive from New Orleans to Destrehan and decided to go where the ferry would have docked, but nothing looked familiar to her. The nightmare wasn't specific about anything except the crime. That and the prior night's events put a damper on her spirit. She wondered if this trip would end up being a big mistake. Cameo hid her disappointment and tried to make the best of it by spending the day sightseeing with Joshua, but her heart wasn't in it. And she could tell that his wasn't either. When they started back to New Orleans, they found a row of motels near the freeway entrance and decided to stay in one of them. Joshua volunteered to go get them some lunch.

Waiting for his return, Cameo turned on the TV, reclined on the motel bed and found herself thinking about their relationship. There weren't too many men who would accept her on her terms. Before Josh, when she told men about her vow of celibacy, they would either head for the hills or try to change her mind, but not Joshua. He had respected her wishes and did not try to pressure her. She loved him for his patience and fidelity and thought she could trust him with her life, but after last night, she wasn't so sure.

§§§

Joshua found a Wendy's and picked up a couple of burgers, fries for him, a baked potato for her and a large Sprite for them both. As he made his way back to the car, an attractive woman dressed in a midriff blouse and tight jeans came up beside him.

"Looking for a little company?"

"I...umh, no."

"You don't sound too sure, cherié?"

His long neglected sexual hunger actually made him think about it for a quick second and then Joshua remembered last night's disaster. This was definitely not the route to take.

"No offense, Miss, but I've gotta get back to my girlfriend." The last thing he needed was more trouble. Joshua rushed back to Cameo at the motel. They ate and then he suggested going back into New Orleans.

"We could grab a few drinks, party with the crowd, have a little fun."

"And forget about last night," Cameo affirmed.

After downing a couple of strong traditional drinks aptly named Hurricanes, the infectious party attitude and the alcohol began to lift their spirits. They were standing on the sidewalk and began to dance with a marching band they watched pass, when she looked down the street and spotted a man in black. She didn't know why, but Cameo instantly recalled the shadow in the window and her stomach turned.

She took out her cell phone and took a picture of his profile. Although there was no flash, something must have caught his attention because his head turned and he glanced directly at her. For a moment, it felt as if time stood still and they were the only two people on the planet. She noticed he wore a white clerical collar. Now he's a priest?

Even though he had aged considerably, it was the same face she had seen in her nightmare, the face of the monster who stole her virginity in her prior life. And she saw from the guilty look in his eyes that somehow he knew who she used to be. How was that possible? But she was sure he knew. Cameo felt the world spin and suddenly crumbled to the ground. When her eyes opened, Joshua and the priest were standing over her. Standing up with their help, Cameo grabbed the priest's shoulder and whispered, "You didn't get away with it," into his ear before he stepped away. The shocked look on his face gave her a little satisfaction.

§§§

Her words rocked him to his very soul. He hadn't started out to commit such an ungodly crime, but as the ship began to sink, he became certain that he would die a virgin. It was all he could think of and when he saw the girl, he just grabbed the chance. It was an impulse, nothing more. When God let him live that day, he made a commitment and for the next twenty-four years, Father Francisco Grimaldi devoted his life to God in atonement. When she spoke, he didn't ask how this stranger knew about his one indiscretion. It was divine retribution. Afraid, he rushed away and disappeared into the crowd.

§§§

After Cameo's fainting spell, Joshua put his foot down and decided their vacation was a bust. It was time to go home. She agreed, but only after making him promise to visit a few New Orleans' churches. Cameo was on the hunt.

"I need to find out all I can about the priest we bumped into. Something about him was familiar."

When they arrived at the fourth church, they were greeted by an ancient Episcopalian priest. Although he looked frail, she was struck by his kind, silver-blue eyes.

"I'm Father Titus. How may I help you, my child?"

Cameo explained she was looking for a priest she'd met years ago who had a profound effect on her life and showed him the cell phone picture.

"Why, that's Father Grimaldi. He's been with our church for over twenty years."

"And where was he before that?"

"At seminary, I'm sure."

"And before that?"

"Where did you meet him?"

She knew if she told him the circumstances, he would think she was unbalanced. She hated to lie while in church.

"I want to thank him for the words of comfort he gave my family during a difficult time. It would have been around 1976. I was just a child."

"You don't look old enough to remember 1976."

"My family has spoken kindly of him for years. I only remember him from their stories."

"Well, now that would have been before he became a member of our parish. I'm afraid Father Grimaldi won't be here today. He's spending time with his family, but if you'd like you can leave your information and if he chooses to contact you, then you can thank him yourself."

"That would be perfect," Cameo answered, writing down her name and cell number. "Tell him I hope we speak soon."

CHAPTER FIVE

Two months passed and not a word from Father Grimaldi. Cameo went back to her daily life and immersed herself in work. Things were still a little shaky with Joshua, but spring always filled her with optimism. Soon they would get their groove back.

One Saturday, she decided to try calling the church. She didn't expect to speak with him, especially since he hadn't returned any of her previous attempts. She dialed the number again, doubting he would answer. He picked up on the third ring.

"Christ Church, Father Grimaldi speaking. How may I direct your call?"

"You didn't get away with it, Father Grimaldi," Cameo repeated what she'd said the first time she laid eyes on him in New Orleans. "I called for you," she said and waited.

"Who is this?"

"My name is Cameo Griffith, but you know exactly who I am. We met on that sinking ferry where you raped me and let me drown."

"I...I don't know what you're talking about."

"I guess since you're capable of rape and murder, it shouldn't surprise me that you'd lie, too, and in church, of all places. Guess you can, since you already know you're going to Hell."

"I've repented my sins and been blessed with forgiveness."

"God may have forgiven you, but I haven't. You got away with murder, Father. Don't you think it's time you paid for your crime?"

"Look, Miss, I don't know where you got your information..."

"Is that denial? If you've confessed your sins, doesn't that mean you've also acknowledged them? How 'bout you come to New York and talk to me about it?"

"I'm afraid the diocese wouldn't permit it."

"But you do get time off, don't you? How 'bout we meet on the night of our Savior's birth in a public place? Say, the Trinity Episcopal Church?"

"You won't leave me alone unless I do, will you?"

"I would hope your conscience bothers you more than I ever could."

"And we'll settle everything, once and for all?"

"Yes, Father, Christmas morning will be a new start for both of us. So Portsborough, New York, Trinity Episcopal Church, Christmas Eve, shall we say around ten? That will give us two hours before midnight service to come to terms with our past."

"And you won't tell anyone about our meeting?"

"No, Father, I've kept our secret this long. Why would I tell now?"

"I'll be there."

"I'm looking forward to it."

Father Grimaldi resigned himself to the situation. He had tried to put this behind him, but now, he would go see her and beg her forgiveness.

CHAPTER SIX

This was it. Cameo hid her excitement from her family, friends, co-workers and Joshua. It was a perfect Christmas Eve with new snow on the ground and bright festive lights everywhere. She felt like a child, giddy with the promise of the night. But it had nothing to do with Santa coming to town. Tonight, the man who had taken her prior life would pay with his. In this life, she would make him pay. Then she could get on with her present...and Joshua.

She folded up her note and put it in an envelope, dropping it into the box before she wrapped Joshua's Christmas gift. Nothing extravagant, she'd bought a box of condoms and used newspaper cartoons to wrap it in. Her mother had taught her to save them all year to use as Christmas wrapping. "Doesn't make sense, buying all that wrapping paper when you know it's gonna end up as trash." And on Cameo's budget, she agreed. Besides, this gift has nothing to do with Christmas. She planned to give herself to him on New Year's Eve. They had waited long enough. They both had gotten over that horrible night in New Orleans and things had finally mellowed out between them. He loved her, she knew it. After tonight, she would be ready to share their love. She checked her silver Bulova stretch band watch, saw she was running late and dropped the gift on her cherry wood nightstand before leaving for the church.

§§§

Joshua left his family and drove his Harvard Blue '95 Honda to Cameo's apartment. His folks were a loud, jovial bunch and they always had a great time together; eating, drinking and reminiscing. He definitely had the Christmas spirit.

He pulled into the parking lot of the trendy apartment complex and parked in the closest empty spot that wasn't marked "Handicapped." Precariously carrying four boxes wrapped in solid green tissue paper and whistling "Little Drummer Boy," he opened Cameo's apartment door with the key she'd given him on his birthday. Something told him 2001 was going to be a fantastic year.

On the way to her bathroom, he passed her bedroom door and saw the gift. After taking care of business, he walked into her room and picked up the box. He shook it, but that didn't provide a clue. Maybe if he unwrapped it gently, she would never know he'd peeked. He sat on her bed and began to untie the bow and carefully peeled the tape from the box.

Inside, he saw the box of Avanti condoms. She even remembered my latex allergy! Yep, 2001 was definitely looking up. He opened the box and saw the note inside.

Joshua unfolded the small note.

Dear Josh,

Merry Christmas, baby. I'm so looking forward to spending Christmas morning with you. I promise this one will be very special. I have to stop by Trinity Episcopal Church tonight to meet with Father Grimaldi. I need to end this once and for all. No one should get away with what he did. After that, I'll be on my way home to you and we can celebrate the holidays together.

I ♥ u,

Cameo

Joshua's stomach sunk with the realization of what it sounded like Cameo intended to do. *Jesus, she's gonna murder that priest!* He dropped the partially unwrapped box on the hardwood floor, jumped into his car and sped to the church.

$$$

Cameo stayed in the confessional and waited for Father Grimaldi to arrive. It was 9:45 on the dot when she saw the man in black come through the double doors, looking around. Obviously, he was in just as much of a hurry as she was to get this over with. It was time for him to pay. Cameo waited until he passed the confessional and slipped in behind him. She pulled the knife out of her coat pocket and jabbed him in the back three quick times, one for the Father, the Son and the Holy Ghost. After all, it was Trinity Church and he was a priest. On the third strike, she twisted the knife counter-clockwise. Somewhere she had heard that would cause the most damage. Satisfied that her nightmares were gone forever, Cameo took a deep breath and knelt down in the red carpet to turn the body over.

The face that looked back at her was all too familiar. It was Joshua!

CHAPTER SEVEN

Cameo screamed and collapsed next to his body. When she regained consciousness, she looked up into the face of the short, pudgy African American man who knelt beside her. In her confusion, she whispered, "Santa?"

The man chuckled. "I've been mistaken for him before. Even though I could teach Santa a few tricks. Folks call me Iam G. I like to think the "G" stands for Gangsta. Take my hand and I'll help you stand."

She did and it all came back to her.

"Where's Joshua?" Just saying his name brought her to tears and Iam wrapped His arms around her shoulders. "He hasn't arrived yet and neither has the priest. Check your watch. I think something's wrong with it." Cameo looked at her watch and saw it was only 9:40 p.m.

"But, how? I thought..." She could not say it aloud.

"No, you didn't kill anyone yet."

"How do you know?"

I know all, Cameo. I know you've been harboring a hate that has consumed your life. It could end like you imagined or you could take this opportunity and make it right. The decision's up to you. Here comes your young man now."

Joshua rushed through the double doors, followed by another man. It was Father Grimaldi.

"Here's your chance, child." Iam patted her hand and let her go.

Cameo ran to Joshua, hugging and kissing him all over his face until she gave him one last deep kiss on his lips.

"Hey, I don't think we should be doing this in church," Joshua admonished, breaking away. Cameo smiled through her tears and turned her attention to Father Grimaldi.

He began to apologize. "Miss Griffith, I know what I did was a terrible sin. All I can say is a day hasn't passed that I don't regret my actions on that ferry. I was a different man back then. I can honestly say I don't know what came over me, it was as if I was..."

"Possessed?" Cameo finished his sentence and thought about the hovering, dark shadow she saw in New Orleans. The memory sent a chill up her spine.

"Yes, possessed. I felt consumed by lust. I swear to you, from that day forward, I've dedicated myself to helping others and have lived my life following His word for almost twenty-five years now. But I find I need to ask for your forgiveness. Can you ever forgive me?" She saw unbearable pain on his face. They were both hurting. Maybe today was the day their pain would end.

"Father, I don't understand what just happened, but I think this is a new start for all of us. And yes, it's gonna take some time, but I'll try to learn to forgive you."

Iam smiled at the trio. "Well, in the words of Charles Dickens, a fave of mine I might add, 'God bless us every one.' Merry Christmas, children."

§§§

No one noticed the apparition lurking in a dark corner at the back of the sanctuary near the church nursery. He watched them innocently rejoice in their own little Christmas miracle, oblivious of his presence. Their short-lived pleasure and the prospect of snatching it all away delighted him. He wondered why the "be-all-see-all" Iam acted unaware of his presence, but then maybe He was just waiting for it all to play out, the way He sometimes had a tendency to do. It didn't matter. After pursuing her through several lifetimes, he refused to be cheated.

"Enjoy the moment, little one, but it isn't over yet, not by a long shot." He whispered the promise and ran his gray, dry tongue across his non-existent lips in anticipation.

MURDER IN THE SANCTUARY
a HIGHSMITH HOOKS

I had no idea the splash would be so loud, I thought as I stared at the lifeless corpse floating face down in the baptismal pool.

I couldn't believe what I'd done.

How did this happen? Why did I even come here?

If only I hadn't.

He was a drunk and I had killed him. No way around it.

One sharp blow to the head and it was done. A second for good measure, and my voracious appetite for revenge had been fully sated.

"Oh well, a life for a life," I said, shrugging my shoulders and getting my justification ready in case I was ever asked. The words echoed in my mind like a beautiful Christmas cantata.

Droplets of blood trickled from the open wound at first, but then stopped altogether. Within a few short minutes, a faint crimson halo began to form around the dead man's head. His face was totally submerged, and only the back side of his body was showing. His arms floated to the surface and stretched out on either side, making his body resemble a "T" shape. A tiny clump of dried blood was barely visible, marking the precise spot where I had struck him.

I was a killer now and there was no turning back.

In my panic, I dropped the murder weapon and ran from the chancel. Then I descended a few steps, landing on the main floor of the church. After making my way down the center aisle, I hurriedly sped towards the heavy double doors through which the dead man and I had both passed. I was turning to leave the building when I felt a light hand in the center of my back.

"Excuse me, Miss," a voice said. "Leaving so soon?"

I briefly turned around and spoke to him.

"I did exactly what I came here to do, so now I'm leaving." I threw my elbow back to ensure the man didn't touch me again. He continued talking.

"Did you come here to pray and seek blessings for the holidays? Many do this time of the year, you know."

"Well, not me," I said. "Actually, I came here to seek revenge, and fortunately, I found it. Although I can think of at least one person who might disagree and consider it his *misfortune*," I said with a smirk. "As for blessings, I really wouldn't know much about those. Sadly, I haven't had any lately."

"Then perhaps it is forgiveness you seek. Is there something you need to be forgiven for? Something you regret?"

"I've never been one for regrets," I told him. "I don't believe in them."

"So tell me, what happened here?" the man asked.

There was something about his manner that drew me back into the church. I went inside and sat down near him.

"His name is Peter. And quite frankly, I'm glad that he's dead," I calmly uttered to the inquisitive stranger. As the words escaped from my lips, I felt relieved, like a hundred ton load had been lifted from my shoulders. I exhaled.

So who am I? And what *really* happened earlier tonight in this holy place?

Well, I'm a ghost from the dead man's past who came here for one purpose and one purpose only: to murder the man who ruined my life. On a night when the world would be celebrating the birth of Jesus, I was left remembering the death of my own son. And for that, this man had to pay with *his* life. It was the only way.

At the time that I put my murderous plan into motion, I had no idea that Peter was escaping more than just the cold weather; he had a heavy heart and was seeking penance for the very mistake for which I was determined to make him pay.

Had I known that, maybe things would have taken a totally different turn.

But...I'm getting a little ahead of myself. Perhaps I should start at the beginning.

§§§

Winter usually comes early in this part of New York, and that year, snow had fallen in Portsborough for the better part of a week. I was at home missing my son while trying to busy myself with holiday traditions of the past.

I closed my eyes. My mind immediately went back to the night Jeremy died.

An eight-foot tall fresh pine tree stood lit and decorated in the living room. Its aroma permeated the entire house. I loved the smell of it. There were wrapped presents stacked around the bottom of the tree that were waiting to be opened. Most of them were for Jeremy. A shiny new bike rested among them near the wood-burning fireplace.

I remember it like it was yesterday.

"Merry Christmas, Mommy," I heard him say. "Are the cookies ready for me to put the sprinkles on?"

"Yep, they're just about ready," I told him.

I gathered the frosting, sprinkles, and wax paper.

"Don't forget we're taking some to Grandpa Jack's tomorrow," Jeremy reminded me.

"Well, you'd better hurry up before the snowmen jump off the cookie sheet and make a run for it," I told him. "If that happens, you may not have enough cookies left for your grandpa or anyone else."

"And then can I open one present early, Mom? Can I, can I?" he begged.

"Absolutely not," I said.

"Please, Mom? It's *almost* Christmas."

"You already know what one gift is. See that big bike over there? It's open."

"That doesn't count. Besides, whoever heard of wrapping a bike, Mom?"

"Alright. You got me. You can open *one* present after we decorate the cookies," I said while motioning with one finger in the air. "And then we have to go into town. Cookies might work for you, but your grandfather will be expecting something a little more special from me."

"Yay!" Jeremy screamed while jumping up and down, "I already know which one I wanna' open," he said.

"After the cookies. Now, go wash your hands."

He hurried off to the bathroom and quickly returned.

"All clean," he said, holding his hands out to show what a good job he'd done.

"Looks like we're ready to put sprinkles on some cookies," I said.

Jeremy sat down at the countertop to begin work on what he called his 'Christmas Creations.'

We spent almost an hour dressing up Santa Claus, snowmen, and sugar cookies shaped like gingerbread men. Jeremy put the finishing touches on the snowflakes and Christmas trees.

"That's the last one," he said. Then he jumped down from the kitchen island and ran towards the Christmas tree.

"Hey, slow down," I warned. "And remember...*one* gift, so you better make it a good one!"

"I'll bet they're all good ones, Mom, 'cause you're so awesome!"

"Can't argue with that," I said with a smile.

The next thing I heard was wrapping paper being ripped to shreds in an anxious child's frenzy.

"Awwww, cool!" my son screamed as he came running back into the kitchen. "A Nerf gun. Exactly what I wanted! You're the best, Mom!"

"I'll expect plenty of hugs for the next year," I told him. "Okay, now get your coat. Remember, the deal was one gift, and then we have to do a little last-minute shopping."

Jeremy darted off. "Mom, can I....."

"And no Nerf guns in the car," I said before he could finish his question. "It'll be here when we get back.

When we get back, I thought. Tears welled up in my eyes just from saying the words.

We eventually made it downtown, parked the car and started walking towards Main Street.

As Jeremy and I roamed the streets like jolly elves excited about Christmas, all the signs of the season were in full effect: decorated buildings with beautiful displays, shoppers carrying more bags than their arms could hold and people driving through town in cars with those silly reindeer antlers clipped to the windows.

"Look, Mom, it's a reindeer mobile!" He pulled away from me.

"Jeremy, hold my hand. There are lots of people out tonight. I need you to stay right here next to me, got it?"

"Okay, Mom," he said. "Can we go to the train store, look at the trains? Please?"

"We should have time before the stores close. If you're good and I'm able to do what I need to do, I don't see why not."

"Yay!" Jeremy said, doing his trademark happy dance.

Our first stop was the jewelry store. I needed to pick up the pocket watch that I had bought for my dad. It was being engraved.

"Hello. Are you here for that item you ordered?" the young sales clerk asked me.

"Yes, we are," I said.

"Is this little Jeremy?" he asked. "How old is he now?"

"I'm almost eight," he said, proudly poking out his chest.

"Wow! You're growing so fast!"

The clerk went into to the back and returned with the owner. "Here it is," Mr. Fields said. "It's a beautiful gift."

"Do you think your grandpa will like this?" I asked Jeremy as I held it for him to see.

"That's pretty cool, Mom."

"I have one just like it," Mr. Fields told Jeremy.

"When I'm a grandpa, I'm gonna have one too," Jeremy said.

I paid for the special-order timepiece, had it gift-wrapped and we turned to leave.

"Merry Christmas, Jeremy," the owner's wife yelled from the back of the store. "Make sure you grab a candy cane on the way out."

Jeremy rushed to the glass bowl ahead of me. He grabbed two pieces of the candy and ripped one of them open with his teeth.

"Did you say 'thank you' to Mrs. Fields?"

"Thank you," he said. His hands were already sticky.

"There are some disposable wipes next to the bowl," Mr. Fields said.

I pulled a couple of wipes from the dispenser.

"Thanks, Mr. Fields," I said. "And Merry Christmas to you and the family."

We left the store.

"Can we get some hot chocolate, Mom?" Jeremy asked.

"Between the candy and the hot chocolate, you'll never get to sleep tonight. And you *know* Santa won't come by until you're asleep."

"Okay, we can skip the hot chocolate then. Santa's waaaay more important," Jeremy said.

"I've got one more thing to do and then we can go see the trains if you still want to."

"Please? That would be awesome, Mom!"

We walked through the park, stopping along the way to check out some of the craft vendors who had their homemade gifts displayed on carts. I joked with Jeremy that I was never good at any of that stuff.

"But you're perfect at everything else," he said, trying to comfort me. "Especially making cookies and picking out presents."

We bought a few of the gifts and continued our walk.

Jeremy, who had suckered me into buying him a handmade wallet, couldn't wait to put the new money holder in his pocket.

"Can I have a dollar, Mom?" He held out his hand.

I gave him the two bills I had received as change.

"Now I can buy you something," he said with a smile.

"I have everything I want right here," I told him.

"I love you, Mom," Jeremy said to me.

"And I love you more." We hugged.

Since it was getting late, I decided to skip my last stop and take Jeremy to the train store. I wanted to make sure he had plenty of time to enjoy himself, maybe even ride the child-sized train that they have there. I gave him the good news.

"Guess where we're going next?" I asked.

"The train store? Right now?" Jeremy asked, barely able to control his excitement.

"Yep. *Right now.*"

"C'mon," he said, pulling me behind him like a ragdoll.

He dragged me for almost two blocks before pointing to the store. "There it is," he screamed.

Ready to cross the street, we both stepped to the curb just as I heard tires screeching, though I couldn't tell what direction the car was coming from. Jeremy wasn't paying attention and stepped into the intersection with one foot. I tried to pull him back as a speeding car rounded the corner and jumped the curb where we stood.

"Jeremy!" I screamed as the out of control car mowed its way along the curb, clearing a path among the walking shoppers. People scattered and they were screaming everywhere.

I fell down to the sidewalk next to Jeremy.

"Help! Someone call an ambulance! My son's been hit!"

Just then, a man staggered over to me.

"I'm so sorry," he said. "I didn't mean to hurt him." He tried to lift Jeremy.

"Leave him alone!" I yelled. "Jeremy, wake up, honey. Mommy's here." I shook my son.

The man continued to explain. "I tried to stop. Is he alright?"

I could smell the liquor on his breath. "What the hell is wrong with you?" I asked him.

I turned around, looking for my purse. "Did anyone call for help? Where's my phone?"

A woman kneeled down beside me. "I called 9-1-1. The ambulance is on the way."

"Thank you," I said, turning my attention back to Jeremy.

"So he's going to be okay, then," the drunk driver said. "I'd better go." He walked away, and got back into his car.

Less than five minutes later, paramedics arrived.

"Ma'am, is he conscious?"

"I don't think so. He hasn't moved or spoken since he was hit."

"Do you know who did this? Is he still in the area?"

By this time, the man was slumped over the steering wheel of his car, which had come to rest at a pole on the next corner. He had passed out.

"We need to get your son to the hospital. You can ride with us in the ambulance."

I stood there speechless as they put Jeremy on a gurney and loaded him into the emergency vehicle. The doors shut.

Sirens blasting, they worked on Jeremy en route. I could tell my son was in bad shape because the paramedics were whispering.

"He's bleeding internally," I heard them say. "No way to know how serious it is until we get him to the hospital."

I didn't like the sound of that.

Holding Jeremy's hand, I kept trying to get him to talk to me. "You'll be fine," I told him, though I wasn't sure I believed that myself.

A few hours later, Jeremy died at the hospital.

"We did all we could," I remember hearing the doctor say. "I'm sorry. He's gone, Ma'am," was the line that stuck out the most in my mind.

"Gone? What the hell do you mean *gone*? I screamed as I sat there at Jeremy's bedside, crying and rocking back and forth, for what seemed like an eternity.

This can't be real, I thought.

Clutching my son, I spent the early hours of Christmas morning wishing that I could go back in time - do something that would change the course of the last twenty-four hours.

Just one more day with Jeremy, I bargained with God.

But I wouldn't get what I wished for. My son was dead and Christmas Eve would never be the same for me.

I remember thinking that my life was over and even wishing that it would be.

That was exactly three years ago, and against my better judgment, I came out tonight.

Initially, I just wanted to be in town amongst the joy, revelry and those in the holiday spirit. My life is so lonely now.

Bundled up in my warmest coat, boots and gloves, I spent a few hours at the park watching a group of children ice skating. As I sat on a park bench, some carolers came by and stopped to entertain me with their holiday songs.

Jeremy loved Christmas carols. He loved everything about Christmas. As I thought about the two of us singing with the merry carolers, the memories of him became even more vivid.

"It's my favorite holiday," he would say if he was still here. And we'd both be so off-key as we sung that it would make everyone around us burst into laughter.

After a little shopping, I was on my way home. Driving down Main Street, I saw a man walking. He looked very familiar, but I wanted to be sure.

I had to be.

I parked in a lot across the street and followed the man for several blocks.

The quickened pace of my footsteps behind the man made him glance over his shoulder with panic. I lagged back a little and watched him duck inside a narrow doorway that might have been a store, but from my vantage point, I couldn't really be sure what it was. As the man turned, his scarf fell to the snow. He continued walking. A shadowy figure in front of me picked up the wool neck warmer, but did not make any effort to follow its owner into the establishment.

Desperate to keep up with the man that I was stalking, I shuffled my feet in between passersby on the busy sidewalk. A thick crowd of shoppers filled the space between him and me.

"Excuse me, Ma'am," I said, practically knocking down an elderly woman whose hands were filled with bags. Her companion strolled beside her.

"Watch where you're going," the grandmother snapped. "You young people are always in such a rush!"

"I said I was sorry, Ma'am."

While engaged in the brief verbal exchange and fighting my way through the crowd, I briefly lost sight of the man. Suddenly, I picked him up in my peripheral vision. He was exiting the non-descript building that he'd entered. It appeared that he had bought something because he was placing what looked like a wad of bills into his pants pocket.

As he turned the corner, the man's preoccupation with his purchase kept him from noticing me, though by that time, I was actually quite close to him.

"This will do the job rather nicely," I heard him say. He slipped a small brown bag into his outer coat pocket, and then patted it with his hand.

Good thing I didn't lose him, I thought.

Now that we were walking down one of the longest blocks in the city, I decided that it would be a good idea to put a little distance between us. I staggered my steps behind him so that I could still see him, but hoped that he had not seen me. I waited for his next move.

"One thousand one...One thousand two...," I counted before taking a few quick steps to catch up. Then I found myself right behind the man again. A closer look revealed what I had originally prayed for; just as I thought, it was Peter Nucci, the man who killed my only child!

Peter walked several more blocks before he abruptly stopped to pinpoint Trinity Episcopal Church.

I took our unplanned encounter near the place of worship as a sign from God. And *that's* when it came to me.

"Tonight's the night you'll *finally* pay for what you did," I said as I watched Peter cross the street ahead of me and attack the main doors of the church. He walked inside.

I quickly followed and watched him stumble towards the sanctuary floor.

I wondered if he was drunk again.

Peter had struggled with sobriety for the last two years. At one point, he'd made it through ninety-two long days without so much as a drop of alcohol crossing his lips, but one tiny sip at a birthday party sent him reeling back into the downward spiral that his life had become. His wife of twelve years eventually threw him out of the family home, divorced him, and moved to California with their two young children. After that, the name "Peter Nucci" became little more than a stat on the clipboard of whatever homeless shelter or soup kitchen happened to have a bed available or a hot meal up for grabs.

On this night, he was seeking refuge in one of the few places where he'd always found peace. It was Christmas Eve, and he too, was missing his children.

In the solace of his liquor-drenched world, Peter would often reminisce about all of the years that he had spent dressed up as Santa Claus for his large, extended family. His thin frame draped in the red suit with not nearly enough padding, even the kids knew it was him.

"We took a vote and we all think that Santa kind of looks like Uncle Peter," his youngest nephews would whisper, their eyes full of innocent suspicion.

The older children snickered in the background, but held their tongues, having been warned (and bribed) not to spoil things for the little ones.

It was the same scene every single Christmas, but each year, Peter was the first one to volunteer for the job of the jolly gift-giver. And no one else bothered to fight him for the prized holiday throne.

Peter wondered who would play Santa for the family this Christmas.

As he honed in on the rows of seats far ahead of him, Peter was distracted by several stained glass windows to his right. He took a moment to admire the unique design of each one, which represented a colorful scene from the Bible.

I slowed my pace behind him as we approached the floor of the church's main sanctuary.

While Peter gazed at the art, I saw a few other visitors scattered throughout the church. One man nodded as I passed. He continued walking towards Peter.

"Good evening, Sir," I heard the short, pudgy man say as Peter's focused walk took him further up the aisle. "And a Merry Christmas to you." I cleverly ducked out of sight.

Peter was oblivious to the stranger's presence and his well wishes.

I just need to pray, Peter moaned while clearing the way with a dismissive sweep of his arm. He found a seat near the back of the church and plopped himself down. A small metal flask filled his overcoat pocket. Peter pulled out the libations and took a more than generous swig. "Ahhhh, just what I need," Peter said when the drink hit the back of his throat. "Smooth medicine for what ails an old drunk."

Another man in tattered clothes and worn shoes quietly sat down beside Peter, who glanced over at the man and offered him a drink. "Would you like a sip, my friend? It'll keep you nice and warm on a cold winter night."

"No thank you," the man answered. "I don't drink. And you shouldn't either. Drunkenness is a sin."

"Then I guess I'm in the right place, huh?" Peter retorted. "And why *shouldn't* I get drunk?" Peter asked. "I *always* drink on Christmas Eve. It's the only way I can make it through the season. Besides, what else do I have to do? It's not like anybody cares about me or what I do." Peter tilted his head back and chugged down a big gulp of what was left in the flask. Only a few drops remained.

"I'd better slow down, save something for later," Peter chuckled to himself.

I couldn't believe that Peter was still drinking! Hadn't he learned his lesson?

From a distance, I watched and listened to the men, catching bits and pieces of the conversation between the two of them.

"You *sure* you don't want a little sip?" Peter asked the man a second time. A stern nod and angry look let Peter know that the stranger had no intention of sharing a drink or anything else with him.

"Well, don't say I didn't offer because I did. Twice," Peter told the man as he rose from his seat. "More for me," he said raising the near-empty flask to his impatient lips while he walked. His heavy but deliberate footsteps led him to the confession booth. He kneeled.

"Lord, I don't know what I'm supposed to do," Peter said through clenched teeth. "I don't *want* to drink, but I need to forget."

I crept up behind him, leaned over his shoulder, and whispered in his ear. "Well, I can't forget, so you shouldn't be able to either."

He mumbled something under his breath that made no sense at all to me. He looked up. "Who are you?" he asked as if he was puzzled by the words that I had spoken.

"You don't remember me?" I asked in a tone that reeked of the intense anger that had built inside me.

In his deep stupor, perhaps Peter mistook the voice he heard as God speaking to him. Or maybe he assumed it was his conscience.

As far as I was concerned, it really didn't matter. Though, it did occur to me that if he thought I was God, perhaps I would get some straight answers from him.

"You killed my son and now you expect *sympathy*? Relief from your pain?"

Peter's memory was jogged by my pointed accusation.

"That accident was *not* my fault! You should have been more careful and held his hand a little tighter!" he said to me.

"And you never should have been behind the wheel of a car that night!" I said. "You killed my son when you were drunk! Do you know how much pain you've caused me? How I've been absolutely inconsolable since that night? Do you even care?"

"You're not the only one in pain, lady! I lost *everything* that night!" Peter snapped. "That one unfortunate moment cost me my career, wife, and my children. She won't let me see them!"

"*An unfortunate moment*? Is *that* what you call what happened that night?" I was beyond angry at the way he was trivializing Jeremy's death. "You're a murderer! Peter, and because of your actions, my son is dead! Now, as for *your* children, at *least* they're still alive!"

After pulling something from his inside right pocket with his left hand, Peter bowed his head and resumed his confession. I interrupted him.

"Do you believe in God, Peter?" I asked him.

"What?" Peter said, with his face now contorted with confusion.

"Do you believe in God?" I reiterated syllable-by-syllable for emphasis. "You *must* believe, because you're in a church. You *do* realize you're in a church, don't you?"

"Leave me alone! I know *exactly* where I am. And I told you I just want to pray!" He tightened his palm around the item from his pocket, totaling concealing it.

"Get up," I said grabbing him in the back by the collar of his coat. My whole body trembled in anticipation of the revenge I would soon enjoy. We're going to the baptismal pool," I announced to my victim-in-waiting.

Peter did not resist my forceful grasp. In fact, he didn't even turn his head around to look at me. Instead, he slowly began to rise from the floor of the confessional. First to one knee, then he stood fully upright. His shoulders sunk in surrender.

"Move," I ordered him with a nudge. Once he was walking, I was able to control his stride as we headed in the direction of the water.

On the way up the steps, my eyes were drawn to a lone gold candlestick sitting in the middle of the altar. It was beautiful.

I knew what I had to do, and finding that candlestick only confirmed it.

Another sign from God, I concluded in my vengeful, demented mind. I quickly grabbed the would-be weapon from the altar and held it firmly in my right hand. I shoved a drunken Peter from behind with my left hand.

A short walk later, we had reached the pool.

"On your knees," I told Peter, forcing him to the ground. The stillness of the water was an astounding contrast to the violent tide that rumbled in my soul. I had one last chance to change my mind, but I didn't take it. "Now, you will pray for forgiveness," I said to Peter. "Then, I will baptize you and *God* will decide if you live or die."

As Peter kneeled by the side of the pool, music from the pipe organ provided a heavenly backdrop to the hellish fury that was raging inside me. I thought about all the holidays that I would be without my son, how he would never graduate high school, he would never marry and he would never give me any grandchildren. And it was all because of Peter. I began to cry.

"I'm sorry," I said through my tears. Then I gathered myself. "But I have to do this. It's the only way I can make things right for both of us. You have kids, so you must understand how I'm feeling right now. I'm certain that you would do the same thing if the situation was reversed."

Before Peter could respond to my rant, I drew the candlestick back and struck him at the base of the skull. Hard.

Then I struck him again.

The impact of the second blow rattled the weapon in my hand, but I managed to maintain my grip. Peter tipped forward and fell into the water with a splash that left me almost as wet as he was.

Startled by the sound of the splash and the shock of the cold water, I jumped backward from the edge of the pool, dropping the candlestick. In my paranoia, I looked around, certain that someone had heard the enormous commotion, and my first instinct was to run from the church.

But what if no one saw me? I thought. I didn't want to risk getting caught by drawing undue attention to myself, so I slowly shuffled my way past the altar and back towards the front of the church.

I walked across the sanctuary floor, past all of its pews. A few holiday visitors were praying and sitting silently. Others were singing to themselves and reading the Good Book. None of them paid any attention to me. I passed through the first set of double doors completely unnoticed.

Almost there.

Then I felt it. This time, I was the one being followed. I knew it, but I continued walking.

I made it as far as the church's exterior double doors when a hand lightly rested on my back just as I was reaching for the wrought-iron handle.

Keep walking, I told myself. *No one saw what you did.*

Instead, I turned to see who it was. It was the same man who had greeted Peter when he first entered the church. I began to worry.

Did he see me kill Peter? And if so, had he told anyone?

I decided to talk to the man, who looked perfectly harmless. If nothing else, I would find out how much he knew about my sinful deed. And I could always leave. It wasn't like the man standing before me was going to make me confess or anything. He seemed very calm as he interacted with me.

I went back inside the church with the man. We walked through a side door and out into a beautiful courtyard.

"Would you like to sit down?" he said while pointing to a stone bench next to a fountain.

"I prefer to stand, thanks."

"Very well, then."

"You know, it's so peaceful out here," I said. "Comforting." I continued to walk. The man walked with me.

"Is that what you need?" he asked, tilting his head and looking into my eyes. "Comforting?"

I turned away, refusing to answer until I was sure I had chosen my words very carefully.

"I need many things," I said. "Some I will never have. Others I've had briefly and then I lost them."

"So why are you here?" the man said, asking the previous question in a different way.

I saw nothing wrong with engaging in conversation with the man. It was actually quite nice having someone to talk to on Christmas Eve for a change.

He seemed very friendly, and so far, he hadn't mentioned anything about what happened at the pool.

Not like he's a cop who's going to beat the truth out of me. And certainly not while we're inside a church! I thought, reassuring myself that I was the one with the upper hand.

We walked through the entire courtyard.

"Let's go in from the cold," the man suggested.

We re-entered the church and went into a room.

"Pardon my rudeness, but I never told you my name," he said. "It's Iam G. Won't you sit down?" The former stranger pulled out a chair for me.

"Thank you." I took a seat.

Iam stared at me as I sat across from him in the small classroom. My tear-stained face showed the depth of my pain.

"Nice to meet you, Iam, but pardon *me* if I don't offer my name because you don't need to know that," I boldly declared.

"Fair enough. So are you here to recover something that you've lost?"

"Excuse me?" I said.

"You said earlier that you had lost things."

"Hasn't everyone?" I replied.

"Indeed they have. But you've also been blessed with many things. In fact, more than most."

"I don't care about any of that right now."

"What exactly do you care about?"

"I just handled something that's been troubling me for years. I settled a score that needed to be settled," I boasted in a matter-of-fact tone.

"And has that made you feel any better?"

"Very much so," I lied.

"Did it bring back what you've lost?"

My patience was getting short. "Why are you asking me all of these questions?"

"That man that you followed," Iam spoke. "Do you know him?"

He was getting extremely close to asking me about Peter's murder and a more experienced killer would have made an exit. However, in my arrogance and ignorance, I decided to continue the conversation.

My fourth mistake of the night.

As long as you're careful, you can still get away with it.

At least that's what the little devil on my shoulder told me. Needless to say, his wise, angelic counterpart was nowhere to be found.

"Yes. I *knew* him," I said, realizing all too late that my foolish Freudian slip only served to further complicate my current predicament. Iam continued as if he hadn't heard it.

"I noticed that I never saw Peter leave the church tonight. He usually stops by my office to say goodbye before he leaves. Do you know where he is?"

I was caught.

"Sir, Peter's dead. He won't be saying goodbye to anyone. Or leaving the church."

"*Dead*? And you killed him?" Iam asked.

"It was pure payback," I said. Peter killed my son three years ago in a hit-and-run. He was drunk."

"And you followed him here?"

"Yes. He had to pay. He was praying at the time."

"Is that where you saw him? In the confessional?"

"Yes."

"And what did you do next?"

"I forced him out of the booth and over to the baptismal pool."

"And then what happened?"

"I made him kneel down by the water and ask for forgiveness. Then I struck him in the back of the head with a candlestick from the altar."

"Is that when he fell?"

"Yes. Into the water."

"So you meant to kill him?"

"I absolutely did. He *had* to pay for taking my Jeremy from me. He didn't deserve to live after what he'd done and it didn't matter to me that he was pretending to be sorry *now*. My Jeremy isn't coming back. Why should he be here for his children when my baby is gone?"

"Did you ever stop to think that maybe Peter paid enough for what he did?"

"It wasn't my job to decide that."

"What then, was your job? In your opinion?"

"To make sure he paid. It was the perfect crime, because to most I knew it would seem like Peter ducked into the church by happenstance. But I've been following him for over six months, so I knew he would come here eventually. And I knew I could get away with killing him. He was just a drunk, so I was pretty sure that the police would assume his murder was purely random or perhaps an accident."

"But it wasn't an accident. Nor was Peter's presence a mere happenstance, as you very well know." Iam said. "He came to church often. To pray and unburden his soul."

"Well, it seems to me that he had plenty to unburden himself of."

"Did you know that Peter stopped drinking?"

"He was still drinking. I saw him earlier tonight. He even offered his flask to another drunk. It's like they were celebrating on the night that my son was murdered. I *know* what I saw."

"You saw what you wanted to see."

"Why are you telling me this? I don't feel sorry for him. I can't."

"I'm not asking you to feel anything, but you don't know the whole story. You have no idea what Peter went through daily, how he was tortured from within."

"I really don't want to hear any of that."

"Well, how about you just listen and I'll tell you anyway," Iam said.

"Fine," I said as I folded my arms across my chest in defiance.

"Every year on Christmas Eve, Peter does two things; he visits the scene of your son's accident and he comes to this church in the hopes of finally cleansing himself of the guilt that shrouds him during the holidays. He confesses and then he drinks and walks home. The rest of the year, Peter's as sober as they come. He won't even drink the wine at Communion."

It was strange how Iam continued to speak of Peter in the present tense, even though he knew that he was dead.

"You expect me to believe that Peter's sober all year long, but somehow he can't manage to keep it together over the holidays?"

"Peter's like you in that regard. But it seems that his sobriety came with a high price, and brought its own demons," Iam said. "However, unlike you, at least Peter was working on *his* demons."

"Peter *was* my demon, the one thing that kept haunting me day and night. And now that he's dead, I'll be able to move forward. My life will go back to normal."

"Do you really believe that?" Iam asked. "Killing an innocent man will not bring you peace. You have to find that within yourself."

"So in your mind, I killed an innocent man? Are you telling me the man who killed my son was *innocent*? And that I should be trying to get *myself* together?"

"No one is truly innocent, not even you. Despite your misguided obsession with making others pay for *their* sins, I'm quite certain that you have more than a few of your own."

"I never claimed that *I* was innocent, but I had the perfect life until Peter Nucci came along!"

"You made a point to ask Peter if he believed in God, but do *you*?"

"Belief is such an intangible," I said. "Maybe I used to believe, but not anymore."

"So you don't even believe in forgiveness?"

"No, I don't."

"You mean 'not for Peter,' right? But what about for *you* and what *you* just did? You *do* expect forgiveness for *that*?"

"I stopped expecting things a long time ago. And I stopped praying when the one thing I prayed for never came."

"But did you really think you could get away with murder *in a church* on Christmas Eve, one of the busiest nights of the year?" He asked. "And that *no one* would know?"

"I almost *did* get away with it. I had practically escaped when you stopped me," I said. "Had I not turned around to talk to you, I would be home by now. Instead, I'm here having done something that five years ago was totally beneath me." I lowered my eyes to the floor.

HE could tell that despite my anger and having committed such a heinous act, I still had a conscience.

"We need to go pull him out," Iam said. "I'll call someone to help. Father Michael, Father Liam?"

The priests who were summoned came running from the rectory. A third priest, Father Todd, was with them. We all made our way to the baptismal.

"Can you help us?" He asked.

"Yes, Father," one of the priests replied.

They pulled Peter's cold body from the water meant for cleansing souls. Iam saw that he was holding something.

"What's this?"

He pried Peter's left hand open. "It's a picture," he said.

"Why would he have something like that?" Father Todd asked. Iam gave the picture to Father Liam.

They searched Peter's inside coat pocket and found a plastic bag. Iam opened it. "It's a letter and a newspaper clipping about an accident. How long ago did you say he killed your son?"

"It's been three years... 1997."

Father Liam asked, "Is this your boy?" He handed me the picture.

I instantly recognized my son. I began to weep.

"Oh, God! What have I done?"

Iam cleared his throat.

In the typed letter, Peter explained how his life wasn't the same after the accident. And how it was no longer worth living.

> *A life for a life, And now that I've lost everything, I understand the pain I inflicted on Jeremy's mother,* Peter wrote. *I'm a horrible person, and I don't deserve to live.*

"So he really *was* sorry," I said through my tears. "I didn't think he was. But he remembered Jeremy's name. He remembered his name!"

The note continued.

> *I haven't had peace since that day. And while God may forgive me, I will never forgive myself for what I've done. I don't expect Jeremy's mother to ever forgive me either. There's only one thing left for me to do. I know that suicide is a sin, but it isn't my first. It will, however, be my last. May God have mercy on this drunken sinner's soul.*

At the bottom of the pool, they found a brown bag. There was a loaded gun inside.

Peter's plan had become clear: this would be his last Christmas tortured over Jeremy's death. Clutching a picture of my little boy, Peter was going to end his life in the one place where he always felt at home.

"That must be what he bought while I was following him," I said. "I remember seeing Peter put that brown bag in his pocket. But I couldn't tell what store he'd gone into and there was no signage, so I just assumed it was probably a bottle of liquor inside the bag. He was a drunk, after all."

Iam said that Peter's plan was no surprise to him. "I've seen him almost weekly for over two years now and he was very fragile, though he tried to put up a good front from time to time."

The priests stood there silent, heads bowed in reverence.

"Shall I call the police?" Father Michael finally asked.

"Not yet," Iam replied.

"Then let us pray," Father Todd said as we all bowed our heads.

We prayed for divine guidance and inner peace.

In all honesty, I hadn't had much of either one since my Jeremy was killed. And perhaps after what I'd done tonight, I never would again. Nor did I deserve any.

Peter came to this church to take his own life, but in my blind anger and selfish pain, I refused to let him off that easily. I couldn't. Instead, I stalked this man like a predator and when I got my chance, I decided to take his life, his fate, into my own hands. These guilty hands that would forever be stained with Peter Nucci's blood. And not even the redeeming waters of Trinity's baptismal pool would ever change that.

I spent a few moments plotting how I would get out of this horrible mess that I had created.

Fortunately, for me, the so-called interrogation by the happy, chubby stranger had been an epic failure. Sure, he knew all the facts, but so far, no one had called the police. And it didn't seem like they would. I felt like I had hit the lottery. Despite coming remarkably close to getting caught, in the end, I had actually gotten away with murder.

For just a moment, I was really proud of myself and my accomplishment. I decided then and there that I would take full advantage of my good luck and flee the scene of my crime. After all, no matter what happened now, it wouldn't bring Peter back, so it made no sense for me to go to jail if I didn't have to.

Besides, I was the victim here, the grieving mother of a dead child. Iam had to see that.

It was the only way I could move on with my life. I thought, trying to convince myself that I had done a good thing. *I only wanted justice for Jeremy. That's all,* I further justified.

Then I thought of the picture that Peter had in his possession — the picture I now held in my hand. I smiled.

My joy passed quickly, however, and I had no choice but to face the hard truth about the situation: that no matter how fast or how far

I ran, one cold winter night when I least expected it, all my sins would catch up with me — just as Peter's had caught up with him.

I wasn't *totally* delusional.

But tonight wasn't that night, although I wasn't completely out of the woods yet. Not as long as I sat in this church next to the one person who had somehow managed to get me to confess, when clearly it wasn't in my best interest to do so.

That's when, in a split second of clarity and overwhelming guilt, I made up in my mind that I would end the conversation and attempt to leave the church. If Iam or the priests stopped me, then so be it. Otherwise, I was leaving.

As I rose from the side of the pool and confidently strutted towards the main doors, I was surprised that He did not follow me. Nor did any of the priests.

"Shouldn't we go after her?" I heard Father Liam ask Iam as I double-timed to the front of the church with my eyes focused on the door. I refused to look behind me.

Not this time I told myself. *If you look back, you'll go back.*

"No," He replied to Father Liam. "Let her go."

That was all that I needed to hear as I stepped outside the church and walked across the street.

I was free.

"Don't worry. She'll find her way back," Iam said to the priests. "They always do. Life has a strange way of making sure of that."

DOUBLE TAKE
LORNA KELSEY CHILDRESS

Cliffview, a suburb of Portsborough, NY, population twenty thousand was an idyllic, affluent African American community situated forty miles northeast of New York City. The prestigious residents were comprised of educators, entrepreneurs, doctors, lawyers and entertainers. They lived in pristine multimillion dollar mansions with meticulously landscaped lawns.

Life in Cliffview was easy-going. The rich shopped at quaint boutiques and dined at the finest restaurants. Everyone in Cliffview knew somebody who knew someone who knew you. Cliffview offered the lavish lifestyle of a tight knit country club community. Admission to this exclusive prominent group required a vigorous application process. First, the applicant must be recommended by a current resident. Secondly, an application had to be submitted with a nonrefundable processing fee of two hundred and fifty thousand dollars. Thirdly, the candidate must have a net worth of one million dollars. Next, the potential residents are vetted and presented to a five member board spearheaded by the Mayor. Lastly, the applicant was required to obtain three affirmative votes from the board.

Anything less cancelled the application. Cliffview was the ultimate millionaire's club.

Crime was virtually nonexistent. The last documented crime was ten years ago in 1990 when a drunk driver killed a young child on her way to school while she crossed the intersection at Pine and Market. The neighborhood fostered love, peace and harmony. The city's motto posted at the entrance of West Highway Four simply stated; "Welcome to Cliffview. We are one big happy family." December 24, 2000 would test the happy family and rock the city to its core.

A foot of snow blanketed the town. It was unusually cold. With the wind chill, the temperature was twelve below zero. A record-breaking forecast warned the town's residents that within the next twenty-four hours an additional eight to ten feet of snow would blanket the town. With the ensuing blizzard closing in on this perfect picture town, the residents accelerated their daily activities to ensure they made it home before Mother Nature threatened to shut Cliffview down.

Across town near Marlboro Square, the priests at the historic Trinity Episcopal Church scurried about the building as they finalized the Christmas festivities for the congregation. It had been a very busy week at the church as the staff prepared a delectable meal for the congregation as well as rehearsing the annual Christmas play with the children of the parishioners. The priests were arguing, trying to decide who should stay at the church as they all wanted to take the night off so they could spend Christmas Eve with their families.

Father Patrick was the senior church official with forty-five years of servicing God's people, followed by Father John with thirty years and Father Henry with twenty-five. Father Patrick was affixing the last of the red ribbons on the two hundred and seventy five pews, which were arranged in the sanctuary. "Hand me some tape, Father John." Father Patrick said authoritatively. He was becoming annoyed with the constant bickering between Father John and Father Henry.

Father John handed Father Patrick the tape and continued to complain.

Double Take by Corita Kelsey Childress

"Father Patrick, I don't see why I can't go home. The church is decorated, the food has been prepared for Christmas Day services and Father Henry went home early last Christmas Eve."

Father Henry rolled his eyes at Father John and was about to speak when Father Patrick put his hand up to silence him. "I can't believe we are having this discussion. Grown men acting so childish, it's ridiculous. Where is your Christmas spirit? It has always been my policy to rotate the staff so everyone has equal time with their families. I am always the last one to go home. The hour is late and I am truly exhausted. Father John you may leave."

Suddenly, the doors of the church flew open and a brisk wind engulfed the sanctuary. A pudgy short man who resembled a chocolate Santa Claus walked in, humming and popping his fingers to the tune of "Rudolph the Red-Nose Reindeer." The appearance of this stranger immediately brought jubilation to the priests. Father Patrick, Father John and Father Henry rushed over to the man and they all embraced.

While wiping snow off the gentleman's back, Father Patrick shook hands with the pudgy man and hugged him affectionately.

"Iam G. it's so good to see you. I didn't think you were going to make it."

Iam, still encircled by the priests, laughed as his protruding stomach wiggled and jiggled like Jell-O. His eyes sparkled and twinkled while he responded.

"Father Patrick, you know this is my favorite time of the year. I love the hoopla of the holiday festivities. Did you honestly think a blizzard would keep me away? I have never missed spending a Christmas with you and the wonderful residents of this town."

Father Patrick moved away from Him and continued to clean up the sanctuary. "You are right, Iam. I should never have doubted you. You have been with me since my installation. I look forward to our yearly visits. Father John was about to leave, but Father Henry and I need tie up loose ends."

Iam removed his winter apparel and placed them on the coat rack. He promptly began to assist in the cleanup.

"Father Patrick, you and Father John go ahead and leave too before the roads close down. Most likely, your travel will be impeded by the imminent weather. I'll finish cleaning and stay the night to cover any church visitors who might need shelter from the storm. You know we always get a few stragglers who get stranded or need to rest as they make their way to Brooklyn."

Father Patrick patted Iam on the back. "Iam, my dear friend, I am going to take you up on your generous offer. I would really like to go home and continue preparing my Christmas sermon. I know Father Henry would love to leave. He wanted to spend time with his out-of-town guests."

The priests gathered their belongings and prepared to leave the church. Father Patrick walked toward the front doors of the church he shouted to Iam who started dusting the pulpit.

"Don't forget to lock the back doors."

"No problem, I shall not forget." Iam shouted back. "Drive safely."

"Bless you, Iam" Father Patrick said, exiting the building.

He began to roam the sanctuary to ensure all the windows and doors were locked. As he made his way down the hall toward the restrooms, the aroma of freshly baked sweet potato pies, peach cobblers and other succulent desserts permeated the air and beckoned him toward the tasty treats. His stomach began to growl. He decided securing the rest of the church could wait and headed toward the kitchen. He approached the kitchen; his taste buds anxiously anticipated eating the delicious desserts. He clicked on the kitchen light which illuminated all the fancy pastries spread across the black and white Italian marble counter. To his delight, there was an abundance of homemade goodies. In addition to the sweet potato pies and peach cobblers, there were pecan pies, pineapple upside-down cakes, chocolate fudge, chocolate chip cookies and his favorite, 7-Up pound cakes.

"This must be heaven." Iam giggled as he loaded his plate with a sample of each scrumptious treat.

After Iam ate his last piece of cake, he burped loudly, wiped his mouth, pushed his chair away from the counter and rubbed his protruding tummy. "Aw..." was the only sound He uttered as he gulped a cold glass of milk. He couldn't remember the last time he ate so much. He proceeded to load the dishwasher as he began singing "It's Beginning to Look a Lot Like Christmas."

Blissful and ready to resume securing the church, he exited the kitchen, turned off the lights and continued his way toward the hallway located between one of the classrooms and the men's lavatory. He slowed his pace as he peeked into one of the classrooms. Out the corner of his eye, he saw a heap of something lying partially in the hallway at the entrance of an unknown room. Cautiously, he moved toward the unidentified object. *What in the world is this?* " He said to himself. Iam moved slightly closer to the object, which was covered by a white sheet. A cold chill quivered down his spine. Suddenly, his legs became heavy like he was walking through freshly poured concrete. His heart was palpitating at an unusually high rate and beads of sweat began to formulate on his forehead. Timidly, he spoke, "Hello...are you okay? You can't sleep here. Get up and I'll show you to a cot in the Rectory where I know you will be comfortable." He found himself standing at the edge of the white cloth. There was no response from whatever was underneath the sheet. He yanked the sheet away. It flew up in the air and landed in a crumpled heap next to his feet. Momentarily frozen Iam's sensors to his brain connected and the realization that he had stumbled upon a dead body registered. He shouted, "My dear Lord in heaven!" He ran back to the kitchen and frantically called the police.

"911?" Iam shouted into the receiver.

"This is 911. What is your emergency?"

"There is a dead body."

"Sir, what is your location."

"There is a dead body, please hurry. I am alone."

"Sir, I am trying to help you. Please give me your location and your name."

"I'm hyperventilating."

"Sir, just breathe in and out. Slowly, take a deep breath. Now, let it out."

He did as the 911 operator instructed him to do. He regained his composure. "My name is Iam I am at Trinity Episcopal Church off of Marlboro Way. Please hurry."

"Sir, I am dispatching the officers. Help is on the way. Please go to the front of the church to let the officers in when they arrive. Can you do that for me?"

"Yes, I can do that. Thank you."

"You're welcome. Goodbye."

He hung up the phone, quickly ran to the front of the church and flung open the doors. A flurry of snow flew inside. "Good Lord! The blizzard has started. It will take hours before help arrives."

Detective Sinclair Charleston was on her way to work to start the graveyard shift. The weather was extremely bad. It had already taken her thirty minutes to drive five miles. At the rate, it would be at least another hour or so before she made it to police headquarters.

Detective Charleston was thirty years old and the only female assigned to the small Cliffview police department. She was born in Portsborough and was the only child of Dr. Morgan and Celeste Charleston. Her father had a lucrative career as a plastic surgeon and her mother owned a successful high-end boutique and designed her own jewelry. Detective Charleston had been employed with the Cliffview police force for ten years. The last two years she worked in the homicide division. She loved working as a homicide detective in Cliffview because she was paid a great salary for doing virtually nothing. Detective Charleston was unaware that tonight would change her forever.

The static coming from the police scanner started to get on Sinclair's nerves. She was about to turn it off when she heard the disturbing call from dispatch.

"One Adam fifteen be advised we have a 10-84 at Trinity Episcopal Church."

"This is one Adam fifteen. We are about twenty minutes away. However, the weather is extremely bad. We've been notified Marlboro Road is closed. No ETA as to when the snow truck will get out here and plow the road."

"10-4, one Adam fifteen. Is there any officers in the vicinity?"

Detective Charleston couldn't believe what she was hearing and quickly responded to dispatch.

"Dispatch, this is one Charlie twenty, Detective Sinclair Charleston. Did I hear you correctly? This is a 10-84? There is a dead body at Trinity?"

"That's a 10-4. Affirmative, one Charlie twenty."

"Dispatch, I am less than a minute away from the church. I'll respond. The weather is treacherous, send back up when you can."

"Roger, that one Charlie twenty."

Sinclair's heart was pumping at a rapid pace. She was actually thrilled that someone was murdered. *"Finally, I will get to do some real police work."* She turned on her siren and proceeded to the crime scene.

Detective Sinclair Charleston was indeed the first to arrive on the scene. The snow drifts were huge and made it difficult to park her car in the church's driveway. As she exited the car, the frigid temperatures made her move swiftly to the trunk. She quickly retrieved her crime scene kit and notified dispatch of her arrival.

"Dispatch, this is one Charlie twenty, 10-23, I have arrived at the church. What is the 10-40 for one Adam 15? Over."

"One Charlie twenty. One Adam fifteen is still waiting for the snow plow."

"10-4." Detective Charleston concluded her transmission. She pulled out her gun as she trudged her way through the mounting snow. The compacted snow crunched underneath the weight of her boots. Somehow, Sinclair with her status frame still managed to look like a supermodel. As Sinclair neared the building, she observed a person in the doorway. Before she got completely in front of the stranger, she shouted, "Show me your hands. Who are you?"

He instantaneously complied with the Officer's abrasive request. "My name is Iam G., I placed the call," he assured her.

With her gun still drawn, Detective Charleston cautiously entered the facility as Iam slowly moved away from her. I'm Detective Sinclair Charleston. You can put your hands down. Do you think the perpetrator is still here?"

"I assure you, Detective; I am the only one here. The priests left for the evening."

"Hmm..." Detective Sinclair holstered her weapon. "Can we sit down for a moment? I would like to ask you some questions."

"Of course, Detective, follow me."

He closed the church doors and then the two of them proceeded to move into the sanctuary. Detective Charleston surveyed the church as they walked toward the beautifully decorated chairs. The church was more striking than she remembered. The stained glass windows were breathtaking with hues of royal blue, purple and gold. The plush burgundy carpet was a perfect accent. The lit candles gave the surroundings such a tranquil presence.

Hard to believe that something evil had taken place. She didn't attend church; in fact the last time she was at Trinity Episcopal was about five years ago when one of her comrades got married.

Iam G. and Detective Charleston sat down. She pulled out a pen and notebook.

"So Iam G., can I call you Iam?"

"Yes please."

"So, Iam, what time did you arrive at the church?"

"I arrived this evening. I believe it was between eight and eight thirty."

"What time did the priests leave?"

"I don't remember exactly, but it wasn't too long after I arrived."

"I don't understand one thing. Why did you take so long to call 911? The call didn't come into dispatch until 10:45 p.m. What were you doing between the hours of your arrival until you placed the call?"

"I was dusting the pulpit and polishing the candelabras. I started to make sure the building was secure, but I stopped in the kitchen to taste test the mouthwatering desserts. I must admit I was there for a while as I tried everything."

Detective Charleston scribbled some notes on her pad. "I see. So, you didn't notice the body on your way to the kitchen?"

"That would be correct. I did not see the body. I was famished and was preoccupied with the extraordinary fragrance, which engulfed the hallways. All I could think about was getting to the food. I'm afraid I have an overactive sweet tooth. You don't get an abdomen like mine from passing up a bunch of homemade desserts." He let out a nervous chuckle and continued speaking. "Once I was finished eating I resumed my security detail."

"I don't understand, Iam. You are not clergy and yet the Priests let you stay at the church, perform janitorial type services and secure the church. Why?"

"Detective, I can assure you, I am a very good friend of Father Patrick's. I have been making my Christmas Eve visits before you were born."

"I think I have enough for now. Can you take me to the body?"

"Yes, of course, this way, Detective Charleston."

Iam and Detective Charleston headed toward the hallways. As a precaution, Detective Charleston unsnapped her holster and placed her hand on her service revolver. The church was eerily quiet.

'Iam did you touch the body?" Detective Charleston asked.

"Yes... I mean no. I didn't touch the body, but I removed the sheet."

He showed Detective Charleston the bludgeoned body, which laid face down in a pool of blood. The body was partially positioned in between the hallway and the entrance of the nursery.

Sinclair opened her crime kit, removed a pair of blue cloth booties for her feet and slipped on her latex gloves. She grabbed her camera and proceeded to take photos. Iam was extremely quiet as he intensively watched the seasoned Detective methodically work the crime scene. The Detective surveyed the area as she spoke into a tape recorder. "This is Detective Sinclair Charleston, Homicide Division. December 24, 2000, 11:30 p.m. Due to a severe blizzard other members of the Cliffview police department are unable to get to the crime scene. Therefore, I will collect evidence and preserve the crime scene until the Crime Scene Unit arrives. The victim is a female African American. The victim's brunette hair is matted with blood and is covering her face. It is apparent the victim suffered blunt force trauma to the lower left quadrant of the head. Of course, the coroner will confirm. From looking at the wound, it appears a possible edged weapon was used to inflict the blow to the head. The murder weapon has not been found. There is significant blood loss with projected bloodstains on the walls and floor. I am going to roll the body over to see if there are any defensive wounds." Sinclair rolled the body on its back and was horrified. The lifeless body with wide open eyes looked exactly like her. *What the...?*

Detective Charleston gasped, dropped the recorder on the floor, stumbled backward and slumped against the wall. He could clearly see the victims face. "Oh...my!" He cried and rushed to Detective Charleston side.

Iam spoke with great concern as he knelt down and faced the stunned detective. "Detective Charleston, are you okay? Do you need me to get you anything?"

Unable to remove her gaze from the body, Sinclair somberly spoke, "Iam Can you get me a glass of water? I need you to contact Father Patrick. He needs to get here as soon as possible."

Iam got up. I will be right back with your water and I will get in touch with Father Patrick. Is there anything else you need?"

"I need answers." Sinclair slowly stated.

Moments later, Iam returned to the nursery with a bottle of water. He found Sinclair hovering over the body and interrupted her. "Here my dear, is your water. Did you find any identification?"

Sinclair turned toward Iam, grabbed the water and took a swig before she spoke. "Thank you. No, I haven't located any type of identification. I am shorthanded here and I normally would not ask a civilian to help me, but can you search the church to see if you can locate the victim's purse?"

"Yes, I would be honored to help you. Detective, may I ask you a question?"

"Good ahead and you can call me Sinclair."

"Okay... thank you. Sinclair. Is this woman your twin sister?"

"I... I don't have any siblings. It's impossible, isn't it?"

"Sinclair, I don't know. But I do know one thing. The lifeless young woman was just as beautiful as you are standing here today. She has to be related to you."

Sinclair ignored Iam He exited the hallway and began his search for a purse or anything that might identify the victim. Sinclair resumed processing the crime scene. She bagged the white cloth, pulled out her flashlight and turned the nursery upside down, as she looked for the murder weapon in every nook and cranny. Becoming frustrated, she turned her attention to the blood splatter on the changing table. While collecting the specimen's, she dropped her flashlight and it rolled underneath it. She bent down and started to crawl under the furniture. Surprisingly, she came across a bloody object.

"*Bingo!*" Sinclair said to no one in particular. She pulled out a bloodied candelabrum. "I think I've found the murder weapon." The bloodied edges of the candelabra were the exact match of the indentations on the victims head. She bagged it. Slightly pleased with her findings, Sinclair's mind was overwhelmed with the major unanswered questions. *Who was this woman who had her face?*

Meanwhile on the other side of the church, He was diligently trying to locate the murder victim's identification. He walked past the confessional booth and was on his way to the Rectory, but something tugged at him and he returned to the booth. There it was an oversized black handbag. He had forgotten to get a pair of gloves from Sinclair. Luckily, he had a handkerchief, so he pulled it out of his pants pocket and wrapped it around the handle of the purse. He quickly ran down the corridor toward the sanctuary. He couldn't wait to show Sinclair.

§§§

Sinclair finished the last of the photographs. She had bagged and labeled all of the evidence. There wasn't anything else she could do. She headed back toward the sanctuary so she could aide Iam in the search of the deceased's ID. She found an excited Him in the sanctuary holding the black handbag in the air.

He was over the top with enthusiasm. "Sinclair, I found it."

Sinclair advanced toward Iam and grabbed the purse. "Good job, Iam. If you ever want to join the force I'll vouch for you." They both stifled their laughter.

"Thanks, Sinclair. Let's open the bag. Hopefully, we will find out who this mysterious woman is."

Sinclair sat down and began to rummage through the handbag. He sat next to his new friend. She pulled out a piece of paper, but before she could read it Iam anxiously asked, "What does it say, Sinclair?"

"It says, meeting at Trinity Episcopal Church, 5:30 p.m., 12/24. 737 Marlboro Way."

"Does it say who she is meeting?"

"No."

"Well, that's odd, don't you think?"

She was getting a little annoyed at her new partner, so she simply ignored him and pulled out a black leather wallet, which had seen better days. It was tattered and held together by a rubber band. Sinclair removed the rubber band and there it was...her face on the victim's Pennsylvania identification.

He moved his chair closer to Sinclair. Excitement filled his voice. "Who is she?"

"Her name was Allegra DeVonna Chambers. She was five feet eight inches and weighed one hundred and fifty-five pounds. Birthday, December 24, 1970. Wow! That's the same as mine. Unreal, we are even the same height and weight."

He cleared his throat.

"I guess this isn't a Happy Birthday?"

It took a moment for Sinclair to respond. "No, it's not a good birthday at all. This is truly a surreal. Her license states she lived at 1624 Mark Drive, Verona, PA. How in the world did you get here, Allegra Chambers? What did you want?"

"Sinclair, is there anything else in her purse?"

"Two hundred dollars, a Visa credit card, a debit card and a makeup bag, but nothing else. Not even a hotel key or receipt."

He rubbed his forehead and frowned.

"Wow... such a large handbag with hardly any items. I don't think I'll ever understand women's fascination for such large bags."

"Iam, you know what's funny?"

"What is it, my dear?"

"I have the exact purse and a worn out wallet held together by a rubber band."

The stillness in the church was deafening. They sat in silence for a few moments. However, it felt like a lifetime for her. She abruptly spoke, "I need to call my parents. Excuse me, Iam."

He remained seated in the sanctuary. Sinclair had to get away. She ran toward the closest exit and opened the door to a snow covered courtyard. She stood in the doorway and allowed the cold, swirling wind to hit her entire body. Snowflakes bombarded her face. She was numb, not only due to the severe weather conditions, but from the strange circumstances. She took out her cell phone and returned to the warmth of the church. She dialed her parent's number. They had to know something.

"Hello, Daddy?"

"Hi Pumpkin, how was your birthday? Are you at work?"

Sinclair's voice was trembling. "Daddy... I."

"Sinclair, you are scaring me. You don't sound like yourself. What's wrong? Have you been hurt?"

"Dad, something has come up. I know there's a blizzard, but can you and Mom come over to Trinity? I need to speak to you in person?"

"Honey, remember, Mom went to Las Vegas to showcase her jewelry. Her flight was cancelled due to our weather. Sinclair, please give me some sort of clue as to what has you so rattled."

"Dad, do I have a twin?"

For a few moments, Sinclair's dad didn't say a word. Sinclair screamed into the receiver. "Dad, answer me, do I have a twin?"

"Sinclair, I'm on my way."

"Daddy, Marlboro Road is closed."

"Don't worry, Sinclair, I have the Tahoe. That truck can get through anything. If I get stuck, I'll walk to get to you. I'll take the back road down Hemmingway. See you soon."

"Dad, do I have a twin?"

"Yes, honey you do."

Sinclair screamed and disconnected the call. Sinclair fell to the floor and laid in a fetal position, crying until she couldn't cry anymore.

Back in the sanctuary, Iam restrained himself from running to Sinclair to comfort her. Her whaling pierced his soul, but he figured she needed a little time by herself. The church doors opened and there stood a snow-covered Father Patrick. He stood up to greet him.

"Father Patrick, how did you get here?"

"When you called about a murder at my church I jumped into my Subaru. I got to Marlboro Way. Made it halfway across and got stuck so I walked the rest of the way."

"Good Lord Father Patrick! That was a couple of miles. No wonder you look like the abominable snowman. I'll fetch you some hot apple cider."

"Thank you, my friend. I'm soaked. I have some extra clothes in the Rectory. Be right back, I'm going to change."

Iam and Father Patrick went their separate ways. Father Patrick quickly dressed and went to the kitchen to retrieve his apple cider. He had just poured the hot beverage. He handed Father Patrick the cup. Father Patrick was about to take a sip of the cider when he turned to exit the kitchen. He was stunned as he saw a discombobulated Sinclair. Father Patrick abruptly dropped the cup and it crashed to the floor.

Iam rushed to his side. "Father Patrick, are you okay? Here sit down. The color has drained from your face."

Unable to speak and keeping his eyes on Sinclair he sat on the bar stool he watched Sinclair walk over to him and extend her hand as she spoke. "Father Patrick, I am Detective Sinclair Charleston, Homicide Division."

Quietly, Father Patrick shook her hand. He unexpectedly stood and left the kitchen without a saying a word.

Sinclair was puzzled. She turned her attention to Iam. "What's wrong with your friend? He looked like he'd seen a ghost."

He rubbed his brow. "Perhaps the two of you previously met? Cliffview is a relatively small community."

"I have never met him before. The only time I was here was for a friend's wedding, and he was not the one who performed the services. I am certain of that."

"I am going to see if he's okay."

"Do what you have to do, Iam I am going to the sanctuary to see if my Dad has arrived."

"Your Dad is coming here?"

"Yes, he is. He admitted I was a twin. He is coming to explain."

"I see."

Iam and Sinclair left the kitchen. As Iam reached the Rectory, he heard Father Patrick on the phone. Unbeknownst to him, Father Patrick had accidently placed the call on speaker.

"I'm telling you. You need to get here. Her twin is investigating the case. This is a mess."

The unidentified man on the other end of the line spoke. "Calm down Patrick. You are getting way ahead of yourself. Did she interrogate you?"

"No...she didn't get a chance to. I almost passed out when I saw her. Get here now!"

"You do know, Patrick, that there is a blizzard."

"I can't keep secrets anymore. I don't care how you get here. Start walking now."

"I'll get there. If you know what's good for you, you'll keep your damn mouth shut!"

Iam walked in the Rectory, as Father Patrick abruptly ended the phone call.

Alone, Sinclair sat in the sanctuary waiting for her father's arrival. Preoccupied with her thoughts, she didn't hear him enter.

"Sinclair."

"Daddy."

She ran and embraced her father. Overcome with confusion and grief, she wept in his arms. Her dad held her and caressed her gently. For a moment, they cried together. She pulled away from him with questioning eyes.

Morgan Charleston was a handsome man, some would call him gorgeous. His well-built six foot five inch frame, coupled with flawless mocha chocolate skin, chiseled features and hazel eyes made him striking. He was Sinclair's hero and she idolized him. One day, she hoped to marry a man who had the enduring qualities of her daddy. A hardworking, honest, trustworthy provider who put his family's needs first, but tonight she wondered if her hero was about to fall from grace.

"Come sit next to me, Sinclair."

"Daddy, my sister is lying dead in this church. Why didn't you tell me I had a twin sister? Did you and mom give Allegra away for some absurd reason?"

"Oh...no Sinclair, where do I start?"

"Start at the beginning, Daddy, you can't back down now." Sinclair said through stifled tears.

"Well... your mom and I wanted children, but we found out she was unable to conceive due to multiple fibroid cysts. She had to have a complete hysterectomy. We were crushed."

"Why, Daddy, why didn't you tell me this sooner?"

"It never seemed like there was a right time."

"Damn, Daddy. I am thirty years old. Hysterically, Sinclair shouted at her father. Are you honestly going to sit here in this place and tell me that in thirty years you or Mom couldn't find the right time? Unbelievable!"

"Sinclair, calm down. I know this is a lot to take in, but you have to take comfort in knowing your mother and I loved you from the first moment we laid eyes on you. It felt as if you were created from the deep love your mother and I have for one another."

"Ha! Comfort...I don't know? Where did you get me?"

"Your mother and I actually came here to Trinity to get some counseling and Father Patrick suggested we contact Saint Bart's Episcopal Orphanage, located on Long Island. I contacted the facilitator and oddly, he had just received twins who were two days old. Your mother and I were ecstatic at the prospect of being blessed with two bundles of joy. We made the long trek to Long Island. However, when we arrived your sister was not there. She had been adopted several hours before. For a fleeting moment, we were saddened. However, when the nun brought you to us we knew we got the right baby. I looked at your tiny face and you smiled. I was over the moon. Your Mom said it was gas but to this day, I argue the fact. I know you smiled directly at me. From the beginning, you were my little girl. My little girl who instantly stole my heart and I fell deeply in love. I knew in that moment I would die for you. I will always be there for you."

Morgan wiped his eyes and cupped Sinclair's face in his hands. Tenderly, he looked in her eyes. "I'm sorry, Pumpkin. Please forgive your mother and me. I love you in the depths of my soul. Nothing and no one can come between our bond. I will always be your Daddy."

"Oh...Daddy, I love you too! It's just that I've lost an identical twin sister I never knew. I can't really explain it, but a part of me feels empty, like I'm missing a limb."

"I know, Pumpkin. I know."

While Sinclair and her father continued to mend their relationship. Father Patrick remained in the Rectory. He panicked when he saw Iam entering the room. *"Did he hear my conversation?"*

Iam saw his dear friend's fear stricken face.

"Father Patrick, what is wrong?"

"Nothing, I am fine."

"Patrick, we have known each far too long for you to lie to me. You didn't even blink. Something is terribly wrong. You can confide in me."

Father Patrick shamefully hung his head. He paced back and forth a few times before he looked up at his dear friend with tears streaming down his face.

"Iam, have you ever wished you could turn back the hands of time?"

"Patrick, I can't believe that whatever you have done can't be fixed."

"Well, I hate to disappoint you, but what I have done is irreversible. I have lived with secrets from others who have confessed their sins to me all the while I have lived with a multitude of sins. Isn't that truly hypocritical? I am ashamed."

He patted his friend's hand. "Perhaps Patrick, it's time to release it."

"Maybe, you are right, old friend. Where is Detective Charleston? She will probably be interested in what I have to say."

"I believe she is in the sanctuary waiting for her father."

"I suppose, Iam, it's a good time to vanquish my demons. Let's go."

Iam and Father Patrick found Sinclair in the sanctuary, still in her father's arms.

Father Patrick cleared his throat. "Excuse me, Detective Charleston; I have some information regarding your sister."

Sinclair wiped her face, motioned for Father Patrick and Iam to sit down. She grabbed her notepad. She was ready to hear Father Patrick, but her father had walked over to him.

"Father Patrick, it is good to see you."

"Morgan, it's good to see you too. It's been a long time."

The two men shook hands and Morgan returned to his seat. Sinclair looked at her father and Iam.

"Gentlemen, this is official police business, so I'm afraid you will need to leave the room."

Father Patrick interrupted her, shaking his head no. "Detective, your father and Iam can stay. I have nothing left to hide. He is my oldest friend and has always been my advisor. I need him."

"It's against police procedure, but I guess it wouldn't hurt. Considering this entire night hasn't gone by the book."

"Thank you, Detective. I truly appreciate it."

"You're welcome. So Father Patrick, what do you need to get off your chest?"

"I guess I'll start from the beginning."

Sinclair agreed. "That's always a good start, Father Patrick."

Father Patrick took a deep breath as Sinclair, I am G. and Morgan moved their chairs and surrounded Father Patrick.

Sinclair grabbed another ink pen and spoke. Go ahead, Father Patrick."

Father Patrick began to let out the secret, which had haunted him for thirty-two years.

"The year was 1968."

"Excuse me Father Patrick," Sinclair interrupted, "but I can't imagine how 1968 has any relevance to my sister's murder."

"Detective, if you will just be patient. What I have to say is very pertinent to your case."

Morgan quickly interjected his opinion into the conversation. "Pumpkin let the man speak. Besides, the blizzard has gotten worse, we really have no place to go."

Sinclair sighed. "Please continue, Father Patrick."

Father Patrick squirmed in his seat. "It was 1968 when a little white girl named Eve Monroe made her way to Trinity by way of Pittsburgh. I found her sitting in front of the church. She looked a mess. Her clothes were dirty and torn. She smelled awful. She was sleepy and hungry. At first, she didn't talk to me. She would just shake her head yes or no. I noticed track marks on her arm. It took three days before she spoke a word and then she began to slowly tell me her story."

"Eve's mother died when she was five. When we met, she was sixteen years old and had suffered abuse from her father. He beat her and shot her up with drugs. One night while her father was sleeping, she stole money from his wallet and caught the Greyhound bus to Portsborough."

"She was beautiful with a radiant smile and the deepest dimples I had ever seen. Her spirit was broken and I was trying to help, so I gave her a job at the church. She kept it clean and ready for service. I provided her a safe haven. She was fed and had a roof over her head. She was content. Until my brother..."

Father Patrick was interrupted by a boom, which echoed throughout the building. Simultaneously, the group jumped out of their seats. On impulse, Sinclair drew her gun and pointed it toward the entrance as the doors of the church abruptly opened. A rather husky man covered in snow rapidly entered the church. He also had his gun drawn. He was shouting, "Not another word, Patrick. Shut your damn mouth or I swear on our mother's grave, I will shoot you where you stand."

"Whoa...Chief calm down and lower your weapon. We can work this out. No one has to get hurt," Sinclair yelled.

Iam looked at his horrified friend. "Patrick, the Chief of Police is your brother? I don't understand. You never told me you had a brother!"

Father Patrick, unable to speak, was transfixed on his brother's gun.

"That spineless piece of shit is my half-brother," Chief Haddock began, "We have different fathers."

Like a giant grizzly bear, Chief shook all of the snow off his clothing. Pointing the gun at Sinclair, he removed his coat.

"Chief, why are you here? How did you get here?" Sinclair asked.

"I got a phone call from my blabbering fool of a brother. He was scared. He got a bright idea he needed to tell you all our dirty little secrets. I would walk to hell and back before I let that happen. It took a while but I'm here."

"Look Chief, let's sit down so we can discuss this situation rationally. Backup will be here shortly." She warned while repositioning her footing.

The chief let out a guttural laugh. "They won't be here for a while. Those stupid rookie officers are still waiting for the snow plow. They wouldn't dare hike up here. I guess we are going to have us a Merry Christmas. I want all of you to sit down. I want to hear what my brother has to say. They say confession is good for the soul. I might as well let him speak before I put a bullet in his head."

"No one is else is getting killed! Not on my watch. Chief. I don't want to shoot you, but I will," Sinclair shouted her warning.

He pointed the gun in Sinclair's direction as Morgan got in front of her, and then he snickered. "Aw...ain't this is a Kodak moment. Morgan Charleston trying to be all heroic protecting Daddy's little girl. Funny, since he isn't really your daddy."

"Tony, please don't, there is no reason!" Father Patrick yelled, pleading with his deranged brother.

"No reason for what?" Sinclair interjected.

"I'm not asking or telling you again. Sit your asses down! Go ahead Patrick, I want to hear what family secrets you were about to unveil." Chief Haddock stood his ground.

He moved toward Haddock. "Tony, you are a good man. Please put the gun down."

He narrowed his eyes until they were almost closed.

"Iam, well, well, well. I haven't seen you in a mighty long time. Looks like you haven't skipped a meal. I have nothing to say to you. You are my brother's friend, not mine. Patrick, I said finish your story!"

Everyone sat down except for Chief Haddock and Sinclair. They remained standing with their guns focused on each other.

Father Patrick was traumatized. However, he found strength to continue his confession. "Once in a while my brother Tony, who was twenty-one at the time, would stop by the church. On one of his visits, he saw Eve. He was smitten with her. For months, I had hidden Eve, but once he saw her Tony started making regular visits to the church. One day, I caught the two of them in bed. To say I was upset is a vast understatement."

The chief was grinning. "Thanks for the memories brother. There is nothing like a young girl to make you feel like a man."

"A man wouldn't take advantage of a sixteen year old, impregnate her with twins and then dismiss her like an old pair of shoes!" Father Patrick yelled at his brother.

Sinclair shouted, "Twins!" as she fell to the ground.

Morgan, Iam and Father Patrick rushed to Sinclair's side.

His robust seven-foot frame shook when he roared with laughter. "That's right, baby girl. I am your father."

"No!" Sinclair shouted.

"Eve was your mother. It's ironic, you and that dead sister of yours showing up here tonight. Happy Birthday, daughter!" Haddock moved in closer to Sinclair.

Sinclair looked at her father. "Daddy did you know?"

"No Pumpkin! I swear I didn't. Now I understand why Father Patrick knew about the orphanage." He turned toward Father Patrick. "You took the twins there?"

"Yes, I did. I thought Eve abandoned them. They were wrapped in a blanket and left on the altar. The next day I found out what happened to your mother."

Sinclair was weeping. "What happened to her?"

"I choked that little whore," Chief Haddock confessed. "She wanted to tell everyone I was the father of her bastard children. That wasn't going to happen. I strangled her and buried her out back, beneath the Weeping Willow tree."

She was distraught and moved toward Haddock, waving the gun around. Morgan screamed at her, "Sinclair, stop! He's not worth the bullet."

She obeyed her father, looking at Haddock with disdain. "Did you kill my sister?"

"Yeah, I did," Haddock sneered. "Somehow she found out I was her daddy. She contacted Patrick first and he made the arrangements for our reunion. We met her out by the nursery. I thought the nursery was a good place to meet since that's where your mother gave birth to you and your sister."

"Patrick left us alone. He thought it would be good if we spoke privately. Allegra whined about wanting a relationship with me. I'm the first Black, Chief of Police. I have a reputation to uphold. I couldn't let people know I screwed a white sixteen-year old girl and she had my illegitimate children. No...that wasn't happening, in this lifetime."

"There was a cart of candelabras in the hallway. I had originally planned on shooting her. Allegra walked into the nursery and I picked up the candelabra and whacked her across the head. I covered up the body. Thought I could come back later and bury her next to her Momma. I knew Patrick was finishing the decorations and probably wouldn't come back to the nursery. I slipped out the back and went to work."

Out of nowhere, Father Patrick pushed past Sinclair. He snatched the gun out of her hands and rushed toward his brother. "You spawn of Satan, go back to hell!"

Screams and the rapid blast of gunfire permeated the once serene church. When the shooting ceased, Sinclair and the others came out of hiding. Everyone was horror-struck as they surveyed the carnage. Sinclair sent a piercing scream through the church. Father Patrick, Chief Haddock and Morgan Charleston were all dead. At last, the sounds of sirens echoed through the walls of the church, but they were too late.

A WALK IN THE COURTYARD

MICHELE T. DARRING

Walking towards Trinity Episcopal Church, I vowed that this would be the end - the end of a long era of torture and pain. I had to release this demon within me. As the church bells rang in salutation of the upcoming hypocritical holiday, I closed my coat closer around me because the chill was agonizing.

I looked at my watch and then at the night sky and proceeded up the church steps. Taking a deep breath and feeling the icy air fill my lungs; I admired my reflection in the doors of the church. I was dressed in my black coat and boots. My hair hung down past my shoulders and my stature looked regal, but I couldn't help but feel an eerie presence following behind me.

Only I could see or feel it, but I knew it was there and what it was. That omnipresence has been with me before. And soon, anyone in the church that would listen would know it, too. Memories of the last time I stood in this church flooded my mind while the nighttime breeze almost took my breath away. Something was brewing and I knew it would lead to trouble.

Passing the church doors, I stopped and dabbed my finger in one of the vessels of holy water that were on each side of the door. The antique look and feel of the gold trim caught my attention, reminding me of royalty and prestige. I was almost mesmerized by the beautiful glistening of the mother-of-pearl vessel. The moonlight beamed through the open door, making this piece of craftsmanship look peaceful and divine. This was so unlike the events that took place here ten years ago.

§§§

My mind started to drift back to Christmas Eve, 1990 when this place was a family shelter. I was an eighteen-year-old single mom, alone with my beautiful two-year-old baby boy. His smile would light up any room and I really needed to see it on a daily basis. It was my only reason for living most days since I was tossed out onto the street by my aunt and uncle.

But my story didn't start there; it actually started two years earlier in a small suburb of Portsborough, New York. At an early age, my parents let me know they loved me and I loved them unequivocally. But one day things changed and my world was turned upside down. I was an average teenager throughout my school years. I mastered in minor mischief 101, but still generally achieved my full potential despite my adolescent decisions. My only weakness was music. I loved to listen to my music, loudly.

One night while doing my homework, I was listening to my Vesta cassette through my headphones. Ballads were my favorite type of music to listen to. Between Vesta and Luther, my headphones were working overtime. I listened to music through my headphones so that I didn't disturb my mom, but also so, I could listen to the music as loud as I wanted. This particular night was no exception. When the decibels on my cassette player were on overload, I couldn't hear what was going on in the house. It wasn't until my door opened and I felt the cold leather glove wrap around my mouth and I was snatched to the floor, that I discovered my sanctum was being invaded.

Taken aback, I shuddered at the thought of what could, and probably would, happen to me. My assailant planted his knee squarely in my back and pushed my head into the carpet and told me not to scream or he would snap my neck.

Tears began to roll down my face and all I could do was pray that he wouldn't hurt me too badly.

He leaned down and whispered in my ear.

"You're such a good little girl, aren't you?"

Whimpering, I answered, "Yes."

He spat in my face.

"No," he contradicted, shaking his head. "No, you not. And your naughty ass needs to be taught a lesson."

"Please, please, don't do this!" I cried.

He shoved my face deeper into the carpet and added more pressure to my back. He had to be at least six feet tall and well over two hundred pounds, but I didn't feel his full weight until he used my head as leverage while grabbing my arms and putting them behind my back. I cried and wondered what was taking so long for someone to come to rescue me from this horrible act. Then I realized no one would.

My body betrayed me and went limp as I gave in to the assault. I knew I had some fight left in me, but his body felt like a ton and the smoky stench of his gloves assailed my nostrils and choked the oxygen from my brain. As he ripped the shorts from my body and exposed the intimacy of my undergarment to his eyes, his hands sought to obliterate his sexual appetite. For what seemed like an eternity, I experienced more pain as he leaned into my ear expelling the heat of his putrid-smelling breath. I heard his sinister tone. "You are going to like this, you little bitch. You know that? You are gonna love it." At that moment he savagely jammed his aggressive member into my resistant vagina and took every virtue I had. As I screamed out in pain and he laughed.

"That's it bitch, cry, nobody can hear ya, so no one will come save ya. You're lucky I don't kill ya." He licked my tear-soaked cheek. "Your pussy is so nice and tight. I like that."

After he was finished with me and both my lower cavities were bleeding and sore, he pulled out.

"That was good. You're so nice and ripe. So now, this is what I want you to do, start countin' to one hundred"

"1, 2..."

"Slower, you stupid bitch! If I catch you looking out the window or trying to call the police before you make it to one hundred, I'll be back. And you don't want me to come back." Chuckling, he emphasized his words by grabbing me by my hair. "Ya hear me bitch?"

"Yes, yes sir," I answered, whimpering.

"Good girl. Now sleep tight," he said as he kissed my forehead softly and left.

I did as I was told and began to count. I didn't want to take any chances that it was a test of some sort. When I got to one hundred, I crawled to the phone and called the police. Since my parents hadn't come for me, I knew something bad happened to them and I didn't want to know what.

Before the police got there, I noticed a red post-it note by the phone that read "See You Again Soon." I shuddered at the thought and balled up the note. When the officers entered my room, I was lying in the fetal position. They bundled me up and escorted me out of the house, covering my head as we passed the living room of what used to be my family home.

"You don't want to look in there, baby girl. Trust me. I got you and you will be okay," the officer said as he took me to the awaiting ambulance.

That was last time I saw that house and the last time I listened to music.

§§§

While I thought of that night, tears started to roll down my face. My heart was heavy and my feet felt like bricks. I figured after dipping my finger in the holy water, maybe if I licked it my soul would once again become pure. I know this is a far stretch of the imagination, but I needed something. I put my fingers to my lips and it became clear the inner darkness was starting. I needed some air. I brushed through the doors I had just entered in order to rejuvenate in the cool night air.

Standing outside, inhaling and exhaling the crisp breeze that swept through helped calm the burning sensation in my chest. I watched as people walked briskly through the streets, not taking in the beauty of the night. They were all in a rush, in a hurry to get nowhere.

"Just rush, rush along now, little doggies," I whispered to myself.

Shaking my head, I rubbed my hands together to generate some heat and decided to get comfortable on the steps of the church to watch the people and cars go by. I tried to regain my composure and my mind shifted to the only family that volunteered to take me in, my aunt, a rigid woman who never really understood me. Because I was a free-spirited person, she didn't like me much either. I was living life the way most people should...with no regrets. Her stern disposition caused most people to think of her in a negative manner. Most people, who knew my parents and what happened to my family, prayed that her energy didn't rub off on me after she took me in. I can't really say if it did or didn't, but she surely tried.

My uncle was hardworking and very mild-mannered. He never really bothered with the troubles of the world. He just prayed that all would be well and done in the good old religious fashion. Although I believed religion had its place, I just didn't see the need to place it in everything. It could have just been my bad perception of religion, but there were so many things wrong with it that I just didn't feel connected or safe from the words most people spewed at me.

Especially my uncle, who to me was married to Satan's sister, if the fallen archangel actually had one.

They say opposites attract and in their case, it was undeniable. With all the venom that my aunt had for me, she loved my uncle with all her heart. For me to actually believe there was some good in that cantankerous old woman was beyond my ability, however my uncle saw a side of her that I wasn't privy to. "Fucking good for him!" I mumbled sarcastically. Funny thing about this dysfunctional nucleus was I don't think they realized or even cared how much their personal neglect of me would affect my psychological stability. But it would be okay because my uncle would pray for me and all would be right with the world. "Humph." I let out a disbelieving chuckle.

His reaction to me after he found out I was pregnant with my rapist's baby was anything but religious. My uncle literally threw his beliefs out the window. I remember being forced to sit and watch him concoct beverages for me to drink hoping that I would have a miscarriage. After numerous unsuccessful attempts and hospital visits, the thaumaturgy nature within him had to admit defeat and finally come to terms with the fact that I was not going to willfully abort the only thing I had left. They both said that I couldn't bring such a monstrosity into the world. I tried to emphasize to them that the baby was all I had. He was the only good and natural thing that came out of that night. I lost my parents, my virginity, and my home, my everything. That was something I knew my father's sister would never understand. So when I decided to keep little man, she put us out.

According to her, "There will be no bastard children living in my house." *How righteous of her.* Sometimes I couldn't curb my sarcasm. Turning around, I had to admire how the shelter had been remodeled into this luxurious church.

I moved around from shelter to shelter with my son. The one we lived in now was one of the better and more affordable places for a homeless single parent. They had a government sponsored program that afforded them the ability to provide child care while the parent went to seek employment or go to work and school. That was really helpful for me because I needed to get my GED. I was intelligent, so it didn't take me long to take care of my educational business. I also had a part-time job that helped me buy the staple items that were not supplied by the shelter. I spent about six months in this shelter and was pretty comfortable with the staff and how they managed the property. The administrator was very particular with the child care division, especially with my little man and that pleased me. She reminded me of my mother, very "all about business," but also sweet and courteous.

The right side of the building housed the child care division. It took up two floors and included the kitchen. The left side of the building was the living quarters for the veteran residents; it also contained two floors, but no kitchen. The center of the building was for new residents, close to the security guard station. Because some families were coming from battered homes, we needed to have security on alert at all times. Until federal funding became an issue, all residents were highly protected.

My little guy, Lyfe, loved to play in the foyer because of the acoustics. His laughter would ring through the entire two stories and bring smiles to the faces of the most injured souls in this place. I knew my story was bad, but some of the families that came through this place really made me believe there was a dire need for this shelter. There was so much hate in this world and I had become a part of it.

I admired the architecture of the building and started to realize the climate change. I really needed to wear a heavier coat, but this one would have to do. In my hurry to get to the church, I grabbed the first coat I came across in the closet. Hell, I was already at my destination and there was no turning back now. With the wind whistling through my coat, I acknowledged the power of the coldness it possessed by blowing in my hands and rubbing them together. Finally putting them in my pocket, I realized that I should have known better than to wear tweed in the New York winter. At that moment, I felt a piece of paper that gave me an unwanted flashback. Knowing what the paper was, I pulled it out of my pocket and unraveled the twelve year old note. "See You Again Soon" was a constant reminder of what was taken from me, something that can never be replaced in my lifetime.

Looking up at the deep, dark mysterious sky for any type of sign or answer to my deepest questions pertaining to my past, I was gravely disappointed to have found none. So much bitterness and contempt, so much despair that my last desperate attempt would be to see if anybody inside this regal statured building would be willing and able to talk to me. If there was somebody in there that had some significant relationship with the man upstairs that might be enough to ease my pain. That would make everything feel okay. I wondered if there was anybody in this big, old building that cared about the person who was lost ten years ago.

As uncertain as I felt about it, I was determined to find out if that person existed. After all, that was my whole mission for coming down here.

When I stood up, I dusted myself off, brushed my hair back and walked back into the church. As I touched the door handle, a gust of wind came and snatched the paper out my hand.

"Oh no," I yelped as I tried to retrieve it from the air, but it was gone. Gone just like everything else.

I turned and walked into the church dejected that I had lost something else. I approached the pews and could see there were a few people there lighting candles and saying their personal homage to the most high of whatever this life was called; however this wasn't for me. I needed interaction. I needed a face to face confrontation to settle this issue I had to disclose.

By the time I made it to the middle pew, my head was throbbing with such intensity I thought it would explode. So I grabbed the nearest seat and just put my head in my hands and sat quietly. Rubbing my temples, I realized the problem with quiet is that it allowed my mind to create its own noise and I couldn't stop my thoughts.

§§§

"Mommy?"

"Yes, baby."

"I love you."

"I love you too, baby."

"Mommy?"

"Yes, baby."

"Are we going to leave here soon?"

"No, baby," I sighed and scooped him up in my arms. "Why do you ask that?"

"Because the man said we were gonna leave here." Those innocent, trusting eyes looked up at me, wanting me to say something.

"What man, baby?"

"That one," he said, pointing in the direction of the newly-hired janitor. I didn't know the man's name right off hand, but I knew he was new because the staff sent out letters to all the residents informing us of changes in the maintenance staff.

"Baby, are you sure that's what he said to you?" I asked, bewildered.

He looked up at me.

"Yes, mommy, you don't believe me? He said you wouldn't believe me." He lowered his precious little head in disappointment.

"Hey now! Of course mommy believes you, but that man was mistaken." Tilting my head in a slant, I wanted to seem attentive to Lyfe and keep this mystery man in my peripheral vision. I didn't want to cause alarm just yet.

"Does that man talk to you often?"

"Only at recess," he said, matter-of-factly.

Now I was livid. *Who was this man? And why did the shelter tell us he was deaf when clearly, according to my son, he can talk and seemingly only talk to him?* There was something familiar about this man, but I couldn't put my finger on whom he was and where I'd seen him before.

"Baby, did he tell you his name? Or tell you if he talks to anybody else?"

"Nobody talks to him and he only talks to me. My son twirled my hair around his little chubby fingers. "Seyas"

"Seyas what, baby?"

"Huh?" He looked at me as if I confused him.

"Seyas what? What is Seyas?"

"The man's name. Mommy, can I go play?"

"Not now baby, I want to meet this man that talks to you. Would you introduce me to him?"

I grabbed my belongings, keeping my eyes on the janitor the entire time.

"Okay," he said. When we got up to confront the soon to be verbally-challenged fraud, my son slipped. I looked down for a quick moment to see if he was all right and noticed his shoes were untied. When I looked back up the man was gone. I remembered the memo said the new janitor's name was Seyas Collins, but it didn't ring a bell.

"Damn!"

"Ohhhh, Mommy, you said a bad word," my son scolded, pointing his finger at my mouth.

"Yeah, man, I know," I answered, looking around in all directions. The janitor was nowhere in sight. "Sorry."

"That's okay. Can I play now?"

I looked down into his twinkling eyes.

"Okay, I'll race you to the courtyard." *I have to meet with the Director about Mr. Seyas Collins as soon as she gets back from vacation. Something's not right about this janitor and his misrepresentation to the staff and I don't like the fact that he only talks to my child. My mind thought of all kind of* unmentionable things, but I shook the thoughts out of my head. Until I had all the facts, I couldn't be sure of any wrongdoing...yet.

When I walked into the courtyard, I felt a sense of serenity. With the exception of the children playing, there was calmness and beauty out there. The landscape was full of magnificent flowers that bloomed vibrant colors. It was almost like visiting one of those botanical garden- type places. The assorted arrangement consisted of golden variegated sweet flags and sutlegen wood spurge, blue pansies, roses and hostas. There were many other flowers out there, but those were my favorite. They aligned the sitting area I would frequent while Lyfe played outside. The grounds even housed a Koi pond for the kids to observe the fish in their natural habitat. It always amazed me with the harsh New York winters how fish could still survive outside, but they did, every year.

On every third Friday of the month, the faculty would have *Reading in the Dark* in this amazing space. The kids loved it because they could come outside in their pajamas with flashlights the staff gave them and listen to all kinds of stories. I believe the kids did more of swirling the lights around than listening. This was fun for them and the parents benefitted because when story time was over, it was lights out for the kiddies.

"Yep, this is a nice place, a real safe haven," I whispered to myself.

While watching Lyfe play, I couldn't help but wonder if he had any of his father's physical attributes. Although that night years ago will never be a blur to me, I never got a clear look at my attacker's face, but would never forget the sound of his voice or his smell. His voice was very distinct and it haunts me to this very day.

§§§

"Excuse me," a stubby, chocolate, grizzled-looking man said.

He startled me out of my thoughts.

"What?" My response was abrupt.

"Didn't mean to scare you. Are you all right? Do you need to talk to somebody?" he asked with a weary look on his face.

Why would he ask me such a question? I was just sitting by myself. Then I looked down. My hands were trembling and wet with tears. This Santa-looking gentleman had a radiating spirit about him that seemed calming, almost angelic. I couldn't help but feel comfortable around him. I wondered what it was about him that made such a powerful statement.

"Uh, well yes, I guess so." The reason I came here just brought itself to light and now it was time to let it out.

"Okay, well for starters, my name is Iam G. And you are...?" he asked, extending his hand to me. I reached out to shake his hand, but immediately withdrew it when I felt the electrical current travel from his hand to mine. I gave him a puzzled look. He tilted his head and gave me a smile.

"Sorry about that," he apologized. "That sometimes happens when I've been walking on the office carpet. I wonder why it happened now. I haven't been in the office today. Hmph." He hunched his shoulders and gently put his hand back down to his side.

"Would you like to sit down or come to the confessional?" he asked.

"No, thank you," I said, shaking my head to negate that notion. "Are you a priest?"

"Well no, not exactly, but I will listen if you need me to. I've found that some people are more comfortable telling their stories to others if they don't know them or are not looking at them. Ya know? It leaves out the whole judgment thing."

"Yeah, I know." I scrutinized him. There was something about him that I just couldn't put my finger on, something very familiar, almost as though I'd known him from some other place, some other time. His hairstyle was in a mini afro and you could tell by the gray that he was no spring chicken. But it had full body and wasn't as coarse as most black men's hair. It was more like soft lamb's wool.

"Excuse me, have we met?"

"No, I don't think so, but a lot of folks around here say I have an old soul, kinda like I've been here before. By your question, I see you feel the same way." He turned his head and looked at me from the corner of his eye.

"Hmmm." I guessed that might be the case and before I knew it I said, "Yeah, I get that feeling from you."

"You never told me your name."

"It's Sheba."

"Ahhhh, like the Queen from the South, huh?" he said, nodding his head up and down with a smirk on those perfectly shaped lips.

I was impressed. He knew his biblical history of the woman that traveled far to ask hard questions of King Solomon regarding his wealth and relationship with the Lord.

"Yeah, that's me," I started to chuckle until I noticed his look of concern. Looking him up and down, I saw he stood less than six feet, but he was definitely taller than I am. His eyes twinkled when he talked. They reminded me of green olives, except they were white, with deep brown pupils. His round belly was so perfect and tight that I wanted to reach out and touch it, but I resisted.

"What else can you tell me about my name, Mr. Iam?"

"Please, just Iam will work no need for the formalities. I know a lot about Makeda, that's what the Ethiopians called her. They believed she was from Ethiopia or maybe Yemen. Depending on who you talk to, her location may vary as well as her name. But one thing is for sure, I believe she was the great-great descendant of Noah. You know, the Arc man," he said chuckling to himself and giving me a wink.

This man has a sense of humor and I felt comfortable asking him more questions, but when I noticed his smile changed into a look of concern I asked, "Why are you looking at me like that?"

"You look troubled." When he reached to touch my shoulder, I leaned back to avoid contact since the last time we touched was electrifying, to say the least.

"I am sorry," I said, apologizing for my abrupt motion.

"It's okay. When you are ready, I'll be around." He winked and walked off.

I started to call out to Iam, but stopped myself. I had to think about what I was going to say to him. I sat back in the pew and watched him walk around the church, greeting people and intermittently stopping to pay homage. So many questions swirled through my head at this very moment. Like *why was this man so nice? Why was he so easy to talk to?* With his enlightening knowledge of names, I had to wonder why they named me Sheba in the first place. But all of those questions would have to wait; they would have to be an afterthought because what brought me here was the biggest question of it all. How was I going to tell him that I killed three people?

This church thing was nothing new to me, but the whole 'coming clean' thing was. I exhaled a long winded breath as I reminisced about last night...

I went back to a place I never thought I would return to. It was a place I had no intention of ever seeing again, especially after twelve years. My aunt and uncle didn't expect to see me, so it wasn't a warm welcome. When my aunt opened the door, I could see her disappointment. She looked around me to see if I was alone and I informed her that I was. Only then did she decide to invite me in.

The house hadn't changed much, just gotten older like all of us. It even smelled older, mustier than I remembered. My uncle wasn't there. The devil lady told me he had gone to the store and assured me that he wouldn't want to see me, so I needed to get to the point of my visit.

"Did you know who he was?" I asked, blunt and unemotional.

"Know who? What are you talking about?" She looked down and began to fidget with her skirt.

"DID-YOU-KNOW-HIM?" The slower I spoke, the more the words resounded through the quiet house.

Seeing my agitation, she sighed with annoyance.

"Yes...yes, I knew him. Why?"

Blazes of fire went through my body. It took every bit of sanity to hold onto my composure until the right time. I had prepared for this day and I wanted to make sure that everything was done according to my plans. I detailed it all, even down to my clothes. My intent was to come into the house looking refined but modest. I didn't want to wear anything too flashy because I didn't want to draw too much attention to myself. But I wanted them, those undesirable kinfolk, to know that despite what they have done to me, I would forever be victorious. I wore black. I like that color. Black seems to have a look of finality, and since that was my desired effect, my Tahari designer coat with the tailored fit and matching slacks brought the *"I mean business"* attitude to this deadly party. I always wear my hair in a ball, wrapped in the back at the base of my head. My shoes were made for the gym. I was going to confront them about the conversation I had heard. If things turned violent, which I was sure it would, I didn't want any obvious signs of assault and I needed to be able to get away quickly without being seen or heard.

§§§

Just days before this encounter, I was pseudo-shopping around the mall when I saw my aunt and uncle. They didn't see me because their conversation was so intense. My curiosity got the better of me and to avoid the chance of being seen, I stood behind a fake plant that was next to the bench where they were sitting. I turned my back to them and started to eavesdrop.

"He wants more money" she said.

"Who?"

"Seyas."

"Fuck him; I'm not forking over another damn dime. Tell his extortionist ass I said no."

My uncle seemed really appalled, and for the first time in my life, he and I felt the same way about something. The last time I heard the name Seyas was at his hearing ten years ago, when he pled guilty to murdering my son. That sick, twisted pedophilic bastard sexually assaulted my son before he sliced his neck open and left him, like he was sleeping, under a tree in the courtyard of our shelter. The daycare called me at work to tell me that my son had wandered off and they had called the police because the so-called deaf mute janitor was covered in blood.

I can't explain the pain and rage that fueled my body at the trial that day as I listened to him explain in explicit detail what he did to my child. His voice was very distinct; my rapist had finally been caught. Too bad it wasn't for raping me. My aunt and uncle convinced me that it would be in my best interest to let it go and not pressure the police into finding him because then I would be labeled and my son would never get a fair chance in life. It's funny how the system works sometimes and as young as I was, I trusted their advice.

I couldn't believe that, after all this time, I would find out my own family had something to do with my pain and suffering for the last twelve years. My body wrenched with pain at that time, but I had to keep my cool until I found out the details of what they were discussing. I needed to know how bad I was going to make the both of them suffer.

"Do you understand what he could do to us?" My aunt's voice sounded worried.

"Us?" A shocked look came across his face. "Really?"

"Yes, us, you jackass. You reaped the benefits from my brother's murder too or did you forget?"

"No, I remember. I also remember how you told Seyas to kill everybody in the house, but did he? No! Instead, he copulated and populated. And two years later, after all that money was spent for a private investigator to find her and that seed of his, he still fucked up and didn't kill her. The only one who could identify him, he leaves alive. That, my dear, is what I remember!" Angry at his wife's implication, he jumped off the bench and started walking away.

"Hey, don't you walk away..."

As her voice faded, I could barely see straight. Something told me to kill them both with my bare hands, but I chose to make them pay and I had a very good idea how. I shuddered at the malicious act of my so-called family. I was about to seek what was owed to me. REVENGE!

§§§

I sat back in the chair and opened my jacket to expose my Mark VII Desert Eagle .357. "So tell me, Auntie," sounding so sarcastic I amused myself. "Do you know what this is?"

"Yeah, it's a gun," she answered, looking like a deer caught in the headlights meeting its imminent future.

"But not just any gun. It's the gun that, after I empty the ninth round into your body, the slide remains in its maximum recoil position so that I can change the magazine and instantly start again. You know what this is?" I asked, reaching into my pocket to pull out the silencer.

"Why are you playing games? Stop toying with me and get it over with." She snapped in such a forceful tone I looked at her, perplexed. *How dare she demand anything from me after all they've put me through? Does she not understand that this is my game now?*

"Why Auntie, are you scared? I know that can't be. How could the big bad wolf be scared of little old me?" Smiling deviously, I realized I was truly enjoying this. Instinctively watching her movements, it was plain to see she knew I was going to kill her. When was the question. But she wanted to test my patience by trying to get up to leave while I screwed the silencer onto the barrel of my gun.

"I wouldn't do that if I were you," I told this despicable piece of a human being, as I pointed the gun at her back. She actually thought she was going to make it to the door before my bullet! *Stupid bitch.* I shook my head. "Tsk, tsk, tsk. You just don't get it, do you? I need answers and you are going to give them to me, right now."

She turned and I could have sworn I saw a tear.

"What do you want to know?" She asked, sounding defeated.

"Why? Why did you hire that man to kill my family?" I walked closer to her and stopped about two arm lengths away.

"Because I wanted you dead! And I knew I wouldn't be able to get you alone, so I did the next best thing. Killing everybody would insure that I got the insurance money as next of kin"

"So you killed my family for money?"

"No, I killed them to get you and the money was a bonus."

"You know I want to shoot you right now, right? As I stand here with this gun in my hand, I want you so dead that I can smell your blood in my nostrils." Holding firm my position, my eyes started to squint in anticipation of the blood spatter.

"Don't you want to know why?" she asked as if the information she withheld was the icing on this murderous cake.

"Sure. Why?"

"Because you are my daughter." she said, smirking. The venom she exuded earlier evacuated its host and traveled its negative energy into my mind, wreaking havoc.

Well damn, I didn't see that coming. This evil bitch was good. I couldn't believe her; it just didn't make any sense. But I wanted to know more.

"What the fuck are you talking about?"

"You are my daughter. I was raped at an early age and got pregnant. When you were born, I didn't want you because you looked so much like him. I didn't need a constant reminder of the pain and humiliation. So I tried to slice your face to pieces. You hollered so loud at that first cut that your father ran into the room and stopped me. Haven't you ever wondered about the scar?"

I was stunned. My dad told me that the scar was from an accident at my birth. *How could I look like some rapist when my Dad and I look almost identical? Oh no, could he be...?* I tried to shake that thought from my head.

"So what are you saying? Who is my father?"

"The man you called Dad."

"But that was your brother," I said, unsure as I contemplated lowering my weapon.

"I know."

I watched a tear run down her face. I didn't know what to do at this moment. I wanted her dead for the murder of my mom and dad or who I thought were my mom and dad. But I almost felt sorry for her because she experienced the same thing I had except by the hands of my dad, her brother. This was too much to grasp.

"I can see you wanting to kill him, but why me?"

"I told you!" She shouted. "You look like him, you are his seed! I hated him and I hate you!" She paced back and forth like a crazy woman. The slight empathy that I felt for her faded. I couldn't take any more news from this woman.

"Walk to the bedroom." I instructed, pointing in the direction of their sleeping quarters.

"Why?"

"WALK, DAMN IT. I'M THE ONE WITH THE GUN." My patience was growing thin and what I had just heard didn't help.

"There is more," she stated as she proceeded to follow my instruction.

"Oh, fuck me, what now?"

"Angel."

"Angel what? I know you're not calling me Angel."

She shook her head, said "No" and pointed to a picture of a very pretty young woman that I've never seen before. She had an uncanny resemblance to my grandmother, but I didn't know her.

"Who is this?"

"Angel," she answered. "Your sister."

"What in the hell?" Another damn family secret! This is way above the normal dysfunctional shit.

"She was first. I sent her away to boarding school. My mother took care of her until she was old enough to be on her own. I kept the picture she sent to my mother so I would know her if I passed her on the street."

"You're such an evil bitch. Open the closet," I demanded, shocked to hear the threatening tone in my voice.

She looked confused, but I didn't care. The time had come and I knew all I wanted to know for now. The last question would have to wait.

"Get on the floor in the closet and cross your legs."

"Why?"

I raised the gun and my eyebrow in suggestion that her demise would come quicker if she didn't respond accordingly. She did as instructed and started crying.

"One last question." I asked. "Why the boy?"

"Because he came from you."

Humph, I guess I got my answer.

"Well, Auntie, I have one thing to say to you..." I proceeded to turn on the TV and adjust the volume.

"See you again soon!" *Pop Pop Pop Pop Pop Pop*

After the deed was done and there wasn't much left of her, I closed the closet door and sat on the bed, reloaded...and proceeded to wait. I heard the car pull up and glanced out the window. It was him. He would be next.

"Babe, you sleep? I got groceries," he shouted.

As he walked to the bedroom door, I could see his shadow between the crack of the door and the floor. I aimed my Eagle and when he entered, he saw me standing at the window.

"What the..." *Pop*

"Hell. I think that's the word you were looking for. Guess I'll see ya there."

I stepped over his dead body, pocketed my pistol and left the house.

§§§

"Sheba?" He said, again startling me and bringing me back to the present.

"Yes, I'm sorry, have you been standing there long?"

"Long enough. You were so deep in thought that you started flinching. So I decided to come over and have you take a walk with me in the courtyard."

"It's still here!" I was stunned and relieved that the new owners hadn't destroyed it.

"Yes, it is. Are you ready to go?"

"Yes."

As we walked around the courtyard, I saw that not much had changed. It was almost a nostalgic moment for me.

"Tell me something about you, Mr. Iam."

"Well, I am a good listener. I'm very soft-hearted because I feel the pain of so many people who tell me their stories. When I communicate with people, I can see into their hearts. I try to help those who talk to me about their burdens in this world, but most of the time nobody listens to me. They think I'm an old coot. So what is troubling you?"

"Wow, you almost sound like God," I observed, letting out a little sigh of humor.

"Hmph, some have said that about me. What do you say?" He looked at me inquisitively and patiently waited for my answer.

"That I've done some bad things and I hope God understands. They say he takes care of babies and fools. Do you believe that?"

"Yes, I do," he said, looking at me very calmly. It rather alarmed me, but I proceeded to tell Iam the entire sordid story of the rape, death of my son and the murders I committed. Out of the corner of my eye, something caught my attention. I looked over at the tree where my son's body was found.

"There is something over there," I said pointing in its direction.

"I know," he agreed.

"You know? What is that?" I slowly walked over to the dark mound under the tree.

"Oh my God," I screamed, dropping to my knees. "Help me! Please somebody, help me!" I looked around and noticed He had not moved. "Don't just stand there, go get help!

The lifeless body sat under the tree, still and peaceful. I couldn't believe my eyes. *Another body under this same damn tree!* I saw Iam standing there, just watching me. It was frightening how calm he was. I couldn't understand why he was just standing there, so motionless and emotionless.

"What is wrong with you? There is a body here, call somebody."

"I did."

"Who did you call? You haven't moved from that spot."

"I called you."

Looking at him confused and unsure if he was the one responsible for this, I started to search my pockets for my phone, but came up empty. I must have dropped it.

"I think I dropped my phone. We have to call somebody."

At that moment, he walked toward me and knelt next to me.

"Look at the body."

"No."

"Look at the body," He commanded.

This was the first sign of authority I had sensed from him, so I did as he instructed. Moving closer to the body, I could see who it was.

"I know her."

"I know you do."

At that very moment, I knew who Iam was. I knew I had seen him before. He was there when I was a baby and she had slashed my face. He was there when I was raped. He was there when I killed my last victim.

"How did she get here?"

"You put her here, Sheba."

"No, no, that's not right. I put that bullet in her heart on the other side of town." I rubbed my head, trying to wipe away the confusion.

"No, you were here."

"Something's not right. I know I didn't kill her here."

As He began to draw closer to me, he put his hands on my shoulders. I felt a magnificent calm fall over me.

"Tell me why, Sheba? Why would you kill my daughter?"

"I asked for help, Iam and nobody came. I asked to be spared and my request was denied. I asked for you and you let me down."

"I wouldn't do that. I am God, Sheba," he said and raised me to my feet. There lies your body, but your soul has been with me. I found you and now you've found me."

After killing my aunt and uncle, I took the keys, got into the car and drove to the shelter. I laid under the same tree where my baby boy died twelve years earlier. The steel in my hand was cold and unforgiving. I didn't have much to live for after his death. Once the truth was told, how could I go on from there? It was sad, the way I left this world, cold and alone. That last bullet had my name on it. And as I pulled the trigger, there was one thing I wanted to tell God before he passed judgment on me. I hope I have the chance. *POP*...and my life was over.

"Sheba, you said there was something you wanted to say to me. What is it?"

"I knew you would ask me why I killed myself and the answer is simple."

"I'm listening."

"Because I couldn't kill you..."

THE ESCORT

TL JAMES

As the early morning rose, the sun beamed bright against the white snow blanketed on the ground of the quiet town of Portsborough, NY. It was the day after Christmas. The town was still sleep and quiet and only the snow birds were out playing and flying around. The serene stillness was violently interrupted by a loud bass booming sound. A flashing burnt orange blur zoomed down the street. The windows of the building shook due to the loud sound and fast speed. The car finally came to a shattering stop after the tires locked up and the car began to skid. It barely missed crashing into the gates of the church. With the sound still blaring, the music amplified when the driver-side butterfly door opened. A huge puff of smoke escape from the inside of the car, as a tall, burly man crawled out of it. Like thunder crashing against the sky, his two feet hit the ground. The shake scared the few homeless people who were using the church grounds as a refuge.

Silas Xavier Luxapher stood at the gate of the Trinity Church. He was on a mission but he had not quite figured out how he was going to carry it out. Iam held a superior place in his heart, but lately things were not right between them. As he took a deep breath, he pushed the gates open. With each step, he battled with holding on to his pain and his resentment for Iam G – I AM GOD, humph. He made his way to the double doors, but he could not make himself walk through them. Silas bowed his head and sat on the steps, patiently waiting for Iam to come out.

§§§

Hours later, Iam stood at the double doors. His heart was so heavy and mind burdened with all the pain from his Christmas Eve experience. Confessions about murders, haunting spirits, vile acts against his creations by his creations, and the ultimate – wishing death upon HIM consumed his mind. He gave so much to mankind, but mankind was still hurting and hurtful. As he took steps through the double doors, the bright sun and the crystal clear sky burned his eyes. He was so burdened that he didn't even marvel at his own creation.

Iam slowly walked down the steps with his mind still spinning. He was so consumed in thought that when he felt a tap on his shoulder, he jumped, exclaiming "MARY, JOSEPH, AND JUDAS!"

"Did I scare you?" Silas laughed loudly. Iam didn't respond but by his heavy breathing, Silas knew he was frazzled. He continued his silent ranting as he walked down the stairs. Silas interrupted him again. "Trouble?"

"There is so much violence and hatred in this world. Mankind is struggling with pain and addiction. Most of this pain is self-inflicted. How are we missing the mark on saving souls? We have lot of work to do."

"I'm working as hard as I can." Silas said in his sincerest voice.

"Silas. This is no time for jokes."

"Why not? You have the sickest sense of humor."

Iam huffed.

"I'm just saying." Silas held his hands up.

"People are taking matters into their own hands like there is no Higher Being. They have no faith or no patience. They are not following laws...THEY DON'T EVEN BELEVE IN LAWS, not even My laws."

"What do you expect? You created these creations in your own image...and with time they have evolved to believe that they are You."

"With your help, right?" Iam retorted.

"OH NO! They do it all by themselves. But I do get the credit. I mean I can wake up one morning around ten a.m. and I have been accused of interfering, weighing people down, wars, gambling, infidelity, even lying." Silas mimicked of fake sanctified voice. "'The Devil is a Lie!' I ain't said shit! They did! But, it's my fault anyway. And they continue to do it."

"Maybe we should start over and..." He said under his breath, yet Silas heard him clearly.

"UT- UT- AH!" Silas waved his finger in the air. "You promised you wouldn't do that again." Silas started pacing back and forth, pretending to think. "Now where was it...it's in one of them bible scripts..." Silas stopped for a moment and joked. "You know if you put all the good stuff in one chapter and named it after me, I would remember these things." He snickered and continued pacing. "AH... Genesis - 8:21." His voice changed as to mimic authority. "And the LORD smelled a sweet savour; and the LORD said in his heart, I will not again curse the ground anymore for man's sake; for the imagination of man's heart is evil from his youth; neither will I again smite anymore everything living, as I have done."

He looked at Silas as if he wanted to strangle him with his bare hands and all His might. But he didn't, instead he kept his stern demeanor and stood his ground.

Silas chuckled and said, "Don't be mad, Twan! You said it." Then he walked away toward the car. He glanced back to beckon Iam to follow him.

He smiled to himself. *He still knows My Word. My most beloved and faithful angel still knows My Word.* He began to follow Silas out of the courtyard. "Why are you here?"

"You know you should've told me that you were coming. Your surprise visits make me nervous. If you would've gave me some notice, I could've made some seafood gumbo, whipped up some oyster dressing, sweet potato pie..." Silas continued to ramble.

He finally caught up with him and grabbed him by the arm. He quickly swung Silas around and asked again, "Why are you here, Silas?"

"You know its Christmas. And I was celebrating." Silas paused for a moment to reminisce about his salacious celebration activities. "Oh good God of mighty, I was four men deep... when your Angels came down, interrupting my pleasures and told me to bring your monkey ass home."

Iam frowned at him.

"Okay, they didn't say monkey." As he approached the passenger side of the car, he paused to open the door for Iam. "Your Grace?"

"You know how to drive now?"

"Yes. Death taught me," Silas answered, referring to his lover, Mallory Haulm. Silas had been tragically forced to kill him by the orders of God.

He huffed and then smiled, "Death, huh?" He walked closer to Silas and grabbed the keys from him. "I rather have Everlasting Life. Get in." Iam walked over to the driver side and quickly hopped in. "Nice car?"

"Isn't this the one you...'saved' him in?" Silas asked, still referring to Mallory and the time that God visited Mallory when he was dying.

"You still blame me?"

Silas didn't answer.

"Is that why you chose to have those people come into this church to visit me? You wanted to show me how much pain you are in? How I hurt you?"

Silas didn't want to answer any of His questions. He looked down and realized that the coffee that he brought for God was still in the holder. "Caramel macchiato? Your fave...I've heard you refer to it as a heavenly drink."

Iam grabbed the drink from him, touching his hand. Silas knew by touching His hand he would feel some relief from his guilt-ridden pain. He felt so conflicted, he wanted relief, but he didn't want to forgive God just yet. Iam continued, "You know Matthew would have fought him forever...letting him suffer in pain. He would have reset life...not wanting to let him go."

The painful thoughts of losing Mallory once again began to build up inside Silas. He had loved Mallory with every inch of his heart. When Mallory was mortally wounded, Silas prayed to God to save him and God did, with a catch. There was always a catch. Silas was days away from denouncing his Throne in Hell. He was planning to repent to God and ask Him to save Mallory so they can spend eternity in Heaven. But he was too late. The Haulm family, along with Matthew's cooperation, pitted against Mallory and created an allusion of Armageddon. Silas tried so hard to protect him, even banishing him in Hell for his protection. However, Mallory was too clever to stay banished or locked-up. When Silas was summoned to Earth to fight, he saw Mallory and Matthew; the Second Coming, in battle. Although it appeared to be Armageddon, Silas felt something different in his heart.

According to the Bible, he was supposed to side with Mallory, Death, and kill off one-third of the Earth. But that day, as Silas took each step, the voice of God kept reminding him that he promised to safe humanity. The Satan part of Silas did many things to deflect mankind from obeying God, but angel part of Silas always obeyed God's law and promises. Thus, that day, went it was time, instead of siding with Mallory – his eternal love, he killed him and ended the allusion.

Silas was still angry with God but he didn't want to lash out again. *You only get so many of those in your lifetime,* he thought. "You know how to get back to Heaven from here?" Silas grabbed the latch to open the door.

"You're not riding back with me?"

"So you can do what? Drop me off at the gates...so I can stand there and watch you as you drive into Heaven?"

"Silas, my son... you can ALWAYS come back. You know that."

Silas closed his eyes, remembering the serene holy feeling of Heaven. The bright airiness of the wind, the many mansions and streets paved with gold. The harmonious sounds of the Saints singing and the birds humming. "It would be nice to return home, to love, peace and happiness. To be accepted among my angel family again." Silas snapped out of his daydream when his thoughts of being happy went back to Mallory. He quickly opened the car door, jumped out and slammed the door. "But there's no sex in heaven. And I ain't for abstinence."

"You can find happiness in Heaven."

"Happiness without Mallory? Are you serious? But then who am I asking?" Silas leaned into the car. "Do you know what real love is? I don't mean worshipped love, I mean real love. NO! You sit on high, looking down. Have you ever had something, been proud of something, only to lose it...to sacrifice it! What do you know about sacrif-" His mind quickly jumped to God giving his only Begotten Son to world for their sins. He bowed his head.

Iam got out of the car and walked over to Silas. He put one hand on his shoulder and lifted his head with the other. "Silas, my son. I love you more than you know. And yes, you are my creation...my first creation, my perfect being." He smiled. "You and I are so much alike that we are one. So much alike... We love...we strive for peace and joy. We show goodness and faith. I have faith in mankind and you have faith in Me. Yes, we are so much alike." He sighed. "I know you loved him and you loved him so hard that when you lost him, you lost a part of you...the part that was your patience or your faith." He paused. "You won't forgive. You don't forgive. You never forgive. And that within itself is what makes us different. And that's what makes me God."

Silas bowed his head again and his tears pierced the white snow.

"Whenever you are ready... I AM HERE!"

THE AUTHORS

C. Highsmith-Hooks has been writing since she could hold a pencil. Her first book, "The Soul of a Black Woman: From a Whisper to a Shout," was published in 2002. The collection of poetry and short stories earned her a mention in Literary Divas: The Top 100+ Admired African-American Women in Literature, a 2006 Amber Books Publication.

After taking a few years off from writing, Cynthia's alter-ego Imani True ("True") collaborated with Dreama Skye on Strawberries, Stilettos, and Steam, a collection of erotic stories published by NCM Publishing in August 2010. That same year, more of Ms. True's work was published in Delphine Publications' anthology Between the Sheets. Both books received 2011 African American Literary Awards.

In the meantime, Ms. True is gearing up for the 2012 release of A Little Sumthin' Sumthin', her first work in the genre of crime thrillers. Several more will follow. Born on the east coast, C. Highsmith-Hooks is the proud mother of one son.

JA Gardener is a writer who loves to read and aspires to be a novelist writing in the crime and science fiction genres. She's also a lover of good vacations and good beer, JA enjoys supporting local bookstores whenever she travels. Finding and tasting local beers is just another perk.

JA lives in Brooklyn, NY with her cat, Zaria, and is working on a full-length novel while she studies for her Undergraduate degree in Cultural Studies with a concentration in Literature.

Linda Y. Watson is the author of the controversial debut novel, Necessary Measures. Linda lives in Indiana with her husband, Elliott, and their two dogs. Between them they have five wonderful children who are all experiencing the joys of adulthood and three lovely grandchildren with one on the way. She enjoys worshipping with her husband and church family. She also loves traveling, reading, writing, dancing and hanging out with her girlfriends.

Since she was a little girl, one of her passions was writing. While her siblings were outside playing, she would hide away in her bedroom where she would read and write poems and short stories. She dreamt of one day becoming a great writer. Her dreams became a distance memory when she became a young mom and wife at the age of nineteen.

But Linda realized it was never too late to realize her dreams and is now writing. She wrote and self-published her first novel in 2010 and is currently working on the sequel.

Jean Holloway's - "Ace of Hearts" The daughter of an entrepreneur, Jean Holloway saw the only limitations you have are the ones you put on yourself. In the early 60s, her father owned his own cab in NY, which was unusual for a Black man armed with a tenth grade education.

Jean's debut novel Ace of Hearts started in 1980, in answer to a bet, yet it wasn't published until 2007. Two years later, Black Jack was released and Deuces Wild was released 10/10/10 on her 60th birthday! On 11/11/11, she completed Full House, the 4th and final novel of her Deck of Cardz series.

Jean now lives in Kennesaw, GA with her husband, Fred and their dogs, Kayla, a Lhasa Apso and Max, an Afghan. Their six grown children all live nearby. They have ten grandchildren and three great-grandchildren.

Jean is now managing partner of her publishing house, PHE Ink - Writing Solutions Firm. The moral of her story: Never give up your dream.

LMBlakely is a native of Albany, Georgia – a "military brat" who has traveled and resided in the Philippines, Okinawa, Japan, New Mexico and Florida. She currently lives in Atlanta, GA and is studying for her Bachelors in Network Management.

She found inspiration in writing by journaling and playing different instruments, composite ballads and had aspirations of being a songwriter blossomed until her passion changed which resulted in her earning the title of "Author." LMBlakely is a native of Albany, Georgia – a "military brat" who has traveled and resided in the Philippines, Okinawa, Japan, New Mexico and Florida. Ms. Blakely is a thirty-something writer, on a writing marathon.

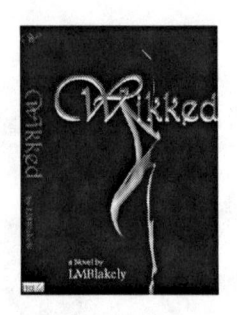

Lorita Kelsey Childress lives with her husband David, in Northern CA. She has three daughters and a granddaughter.

Lorita's first novel The Turning Point of Lila Louise was published in May 2010. She is a member of Sistahs on the Reading Edge book club. Lorita's work is featured in Gumbo for the Soul; The Recipe for Literacy in the Black Community and Gumbo for the Soul; Women of Honor Special Pink Edition. In June 2012, Lorita's latest work will be featured in Suspect; A Confessional Anthology. Her poem Our History is Rich was featured in the January/March 2010 edition of Kontagious Magazine.

Lorita recently finished her first children's book and is looking for a publisher. She is currently working on her second novel. Visit her on the web at www.loritawrites4u.com.

Michele T. Darring, a Chicago native is finding her way in theliterary industry. She is a stunning woman of sheer intelligence andis the former host of her own online radio talk show on BlogTalkRadiotitled The Daring Show, where she was provocative and infuriating. Todate she has over 30 years of experience in using her brain andspeaking her mind. She holds no punches and is very candid and attimes brash in her commentary of current events and social issues.

She prides herself on being genuine and not an expert. Her literary venture has taking off as she has established The Daring Show Reading Club while working to promoting authors. She is also a contributing writer for Voices Behind the Tears, an Anthology about Domestic Violence.

In her spare time, she has written over 15 book reviews for The Daring Show and has been featured in Writer's Vibe magazine. Withnumerous commentaries she writes for her website www.thedaringshow.webs.com she hopes to have her debut novella coming in 2012.

TL James graduated with an MBA from LeTourneau University. At LETU, she cultivated an interest in biblical studies, which became the integral thread in her writing style. Given birth her first speculative fictional trilogy.

As she developed the family drama storyline, her newly born son was constantly tucked around her waist. After eight months of sleepless nights, The MPire trilogy was completed.

James currently resides in Houston TX with her son.

PHE Ink
Writing Solutions Firm

PHE Ink is Houston's Premiere Independent Publishing House created by authors with a business mind. We bridge gaps between large publishing houses and Print On Demand companies. And our primary objective is Getting Books into Reader's Hands.

For more information, please visit www.pheinkpub.com.

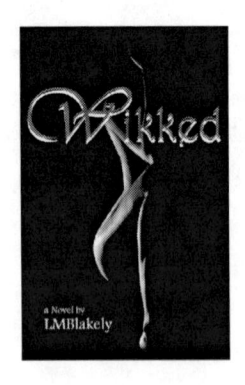